HOOPS Shorts

A HOOPS Novella Collection

Kennedy Ryan

Proofreading:
Kara Hildebrand

Cover Design:
Letitia Hasser
RBA Designs

Reach Kennedy
kennedyryanwrites.com

The HOOPS Series

All in Kindle Unlimited
Available Now

LONG SHOT (A HOOPS Novel)
Available in Ebook, Audio & Paperback
https://amzn.to/2PrMrqQ

BLOCK SHOT (A HOOPS Novel)
Banner & Jared's Story
Enemies-to-Lovers | Friends-to-Lovers | Second Chance
E-Book: mybook.to/BlockShot
Goodreads: http://bit.ly/HOOPSJared

HOOK SHOT (A HOOPS Novel)
Lotus + Kenan's Story
Ebook, Audio & Paperback
http://kennedyryanwrites.com/hook-shot/

Content Warning

Please note that *Full-Court Press* contains themes of grief &
discussion of suicide of a loved one.

Fast Break includes a reference to a past suicide attempt. Not on
page or graphically detailed or depicted.

Full-Court Press

Chapter 1

Decker

I'm dripping wet and almost naked the first time I meet Avery Hughes.

It's my second season in the NBA, and I'm used to conducting interviews at my locker wearing only a towel, with a ring of microphones, recorders, and demanding reporters crowded around me. But *this* reporter, *this* night, from the first look, blind-sides me.

We played a shit game.

Correction. For forty-five minutes of regulation, we played a stellar game. That last three minutes—that was some shit, and as the idiot who turned the ball over repeatedly in the closing plays, most of that shit rests squarely on my shoulders.

Post-game and post-shower, I lean against my locker, eyes stuck to the floor while I duck and dodge the flurry of questions flying around my head. I should have taken the fine for not making myself available to the press. That would have cost me less. This costs my pride and the dregs of my patience.

"Can you walk us through that fourth quarter implosion, Deck?" a husky voice raises above the fray tightly encircling me. "Those last few minutes of the game were pretty brutal."

My brows snap together at the rudeness, the audacity of this reporter. Sure, I've fielded tougher questions, but after this kind of game, a win that slipped through our fingers, and me responsible, I'm too raw and not in the mood for it.

"What kind of question . . ."

The half-formed demand withers on my lips when I meet the eyes behind the recorder thrust at me. They are the softest thing about her face. Her chin draws to a point, and her cheekbones flare out like a cat's, rounding into sharp feline femininity. She looks down her keen little nose at me with a touch of disdain and conde-scension. Her lips are set in a flat, determined line, but that doesn't make them less lush, less kissable. But still . . . the eyes are the softest thing in that face, darkest sable, surrounded by a fan of long, minky lashes. Those eyes lock with mine while she waits. They never lower to scrape over the bare brawn of my shoulders and chest. Don't dip to my waist or the barely knotted towel hanging onto my hip. And definitely don't slide over my legs, still dripping from my shower. Nope, she looks me right in *and only in* my eyes while she waits.

"Well, um . . ." I search for her name on the laminated media credential lanyard resting between a set of perky breasts. "*Avery*, we made some mistakes there at the end."

She tilts her head and lifts her brows to the angle of "obviously" before scooting her mic an inch closer. Her scent, something fresh and wild, like the dark, textured curls rioting around her face, is a high note piercing through all the testosterone rife in the locker room.

"Great night overall. Bad few minutes," I finally answer, crooking my mouth into a smile possible now that I've seen her. "Happens to the best of us on any given night."

I shrug, watching her eyes finally drop to the flexing movement, before snapping back to my face.

Ahhh, made you look, pretty lady.

The dark eyes narrow and those kissable lips part like she already has the next question cocked and loaded, but another reporter butts in with something else. I answer a few more questions, getting impatient to dress and talk to Avery without the watchful eye of every major network. When our media rep shuts down the post-game press, reporters start filing out of the locker room. I consider letting it go. Letting *her* go. I've seen prettier girls, right? I can fuck a different chick in a different city every night. Matter of fact, it's practically my civic duty on behalf of all my brethren who will never have the NBA all-access ass pass. Real talk, I'm already over that. Gorgeous, grasping and vapid. That pretty much describes every woman hanging out in the tunnel after a game. This girl—one look and one question tells me I can't have my way with her. I never could resist a challenge, and when Avery turns to leave, giving me an uninterrupted view of a firm, round ass outlined in her tailored slacks, I know I won't resist her either.

"Avery," I call, holding onto my slipping towel with one hand and gently grabbing her elbow with the other. "Hold up a sec."

She looks pointedly at my hand, so large against her slim arm, like it offends her, before looking back to my face. Some half naked, wet jock a foot taller and grabbing her probably isn't making the best first impression.

"Sorry about that." I drop her arm and flick my head toward my locker. "Could I talk to you for a minute?"

Reluctant curiosity settles on her face, and she takes the few steps back to my corner in the chaos of the locker room.

"I wanted to ask you—" I cut off my words when she thrusts her recorder in the space just above my mouth and below my nose. I push it away with a finger. "Uh . . . off the record."

She lowers the recorder to her side, suppressing what I strongly suspect is a smirk.

"You want to tell me the real reason behind your collapse tonight?" The dark brows take flight over curious eyes and she leans one silk-clad shoulder into the locker door.

"No, I mean . . . I could, yeah. Maybe over a drink or dinner. Our flight doesn't leave until the morning."

Horrified realization unfurls on her face.

"Are you asking me out?" Her incredulous words ring through the room, and I look around a little self-consciously. It just isn't done, approaching a reporter like this. In my defense, most reporters don't have an ass like Avery's.

"Yeah, for a drink or something," I whisper, modeling the appropriate and discrete tone for this kind of conversation, hoping she'll catch on. She seems like a bright girl, after all.

"Or something?" A full-blown frown materializes on her face. "I don't do *'or something'* with basketball players. I don't do anything with athletes on my beat."

"I'm on your beat?" I lean into the locker door, too, crossing my arms over my chest. "I haven't seen you before."

"Well you'll be seeing me from now on because I was just assigned." Her gaze drops to my chest and I make my pectoral muscles jump. She rolls her eyes. "And I won't compromise my professional objectivity with the 'or something' you probably have in mind."

"One drink," I urge, shifting against the door.

"My answer is still—" Her gasp chokes out the rest of her sentence when the precariously knotted towel slides right down my hip and plops at my feet. The sight of my dick, slightly erect and on the loose for all the world to see, leaches the air from the room for just a moment, the total quiet before a storm of laughter and good-natured cat calls.

"Oh, shit." Ignoring my teammates' snickers, I scramble to grab the towel from the floor, jerking it back around my waist to cover up my junk. I've been sharing showers and locker rooms since my dick was half this size, so I'm unfazed. Avery, though, looks like she swallowed her little recorder and it's about to come back up with her dinner. Over the wolf whistles, a leftover reporter adds his misplaced mockery to the mix.

"Getting an *exclusive*, are you, Hughes, your first night on the job?" he asks with a leer. "An exposé? Deck would give me the scoop, too, if I had an ass like yours."

What the hell? I'd heard comments like that all my life. Hell, maybe I've even thought them myself. This sport, this industry, is male-dominated, and we're basically overpaid, overgrown adolescents, most of us, until we've been around for a while. Some of us longer than others. Hearing that shit with her standing right here, though, seeing the hurt and irritation spark in her eyes before she quells it, makes me want to knock the bitch-ass reporter's glasses off his face. Laughter from a few others at his rude comment overtakes any hope I have of convincing her. I glare at the idiot already on his way out the door.

"Thanks a lot, asshole," she mutters, jerkily adjusting the bag on her shoulder.

"Yeah," I agree, shaking my head. "He's a piece of work."

"I meant *you*," she says, exasperation evident in her tone. "You're the asshole."

"Me?" I thrust my thumb into my naked chest. "What'd I do?"

"Could you just . . ." she sputters, and gestures in the general area of my groin. "Hold onto your little towel? Those are my colleagues. Do you have any idea how hard it is for a woman in this field? To earn their respect as an equal?"

My mouth opens to commiserate, but I never get the chance.

"The answer is no," she barrels over my would-be response. "You have no idea because you've been catered to and coddled since you made your first triple-double in high school. Those other reporters don't have to worry about being pinched or grabbed on the sly. It doesn't bother them conducting interviews with half-naked men, which I don't mind either until one of them pulls me into a corner and asks for a drink *'or something.'*"

I let those words sink into the quiet that collects around us after her diatribe. By any reasonable measure, this would be considered a rough start, but I've never met a woman who could resist my charm, my smile, my good humor. My tanned half-naked body. If I'm a betting man, I don't think Avery can either.

"Soooooo . . . you've been following me since high school?" I break out my fail-proof grin. "That's really flattering. I didn't realize you were a fan."

"I'm not a fan," she snaps. "And if I were I'd be pretty disappointed with your sorry performance on the floor tonight."

"Hey now." My grin slips. "You don't have to get personal. That's my career we're talking about."

She turns to leave, tossing the last words over her shoulder. "And this is mine."

I stand there like an idiot, thinking of all the ways I could arrange to meet her. I'm sure I'll see her on the regular from now on if she's assigned to this beat. I dry the last of the water from my aching body and pull on my T-shirt and sweats before I head to the hotel alone. I'm not worried that it didn't happen for Avery and me tonight.

Maybe I'm being cocky, but I'm sure it won't take long.

It never does.

Chapter 2

Avery

T en Years Later

"I'M CONVINCED the fundamental problem of society is technology evolves much faster than the male brain."

I aim the words at my producer and best friend Sadie, meeting her eyes over my iPad.

"How else do you explain dick pic scandals?" I ask. "Something as simple as *not* sending pictures of your dick because it could cost you an election, a career, a marriage—men just cannot grasp. It's like this ancient urge to prove who has the bigger dick. Only instead of pissing on things, they send images of their penises into the ether."

I point to yet another post about my co-host's JunkGate. "I thought Gary was smarter than this."

Sadie walks to the desk and peers over my shoulder at the screen.

"I thought Gary was *bigger* than this," she says.

Our inelegant snorts meet in the quiet of my office.

"I had my suspicions." I set the iPad down and whirl my seat around a few times. "He's got that look small-dick men always have."

"What look do men with small dicks have?"

"Girl, if you've never seen it," I say, stopping my spinning chair long enough to offer a wry grin. "Count yourself lucky."

"As much as I'm enjoying all this girl talk at Gary's expense," Sadie says, dark eyes sobering in her pretty face. "We need to discuss what this means for *Twofer*."

"They're not firing him from the show, are they?" I stop grinning and grip the edge of my desk. "I mean, yeah. It's bad and indiscrete and embarrassing, but surely not a fire-able offense."

"No, not firing, but it does violate the conduct clause in his contract, and it's not his first time." Sadie leans back in the seat across from me, linking her hands over her stomach. "And it's definitely a distraction the show doesn't need, so they're suspending him for three weeks."

"I figured as much. I hope, for his sake, it was worth it." A rueful grin pulls one corner of my mouth back into humor briefly before uncertainty drags it back down. "So how will we handle his absence? Rotating guest hosts? Me solo?"

"Not solo. *Twofer's* popularity is built on the back and forth of opposing perspectives. We need a guest host, just while Gary's gone." Sadie shakes her head and leans forward to grab and munch some of the salted seaweed I was snacking on before she arrived. "This stuff tastes like literal shit. You're aware?"

"Focus. You can't just say I'm getting some guest host and not tell me who, like right away. Who is it?"

"Someone the audience will love tuning in to see."

"Who?"

"Someone credible."

"Who, Sadie?"

"Someone handsome."

"What's handsome got to do with journalism?"

Sadie slants me a knowing look. It's not just journalism. It's *tele-*

vision, and looks mean a lot too often even in sports. I have enough firsthand experience with producers' requests and standards to understand the look she's giving me. When we first started the show two years ago, SportsCo executives asked me to "consider" pressing my hair for a more "polished" look and said they "loved my weight" just where it was. I doubt very seriously they had those conversations with my male co-host.

"Okay. You're right. Looks count," I concede. "So he's handsome. Who?"

"Retired. He's a future Hall of Famer," Sadie mumbles around a mouthful of the seaweed she insists is vile.

"Which sport?" I ask cautiously. Some retired athlete coming on my show who doesn't know jack shit about not just *playing* sports, but analyzing them, debating them, covering them is not what I need on set.

"We're playing ba-sket-baaaaaall," Sadie sings the famous Kurtis Blow refrain

and seesaws her shoulders.

Hmmm. Credible. Handsome. Basketball. Retired. Future Hall of Famer.

"No!" The word cannons from my mouth with fire power. "Not—"

"Mack Decker," Sadie finishes, her smile satisfied. "We got Mack Decker."

"Then un-get Mack Decker." I stand and pace, my go-to when something bothers me intensely, as the worn path in front of my desk attests. "He's arrogant, conceited, self-important—"

"Is this about that towel incident?" Sadie's evil grin hopes it is.

"That was ten years ago. Of course not."

Sadie's steady stare bores holes into my face.

"Okay, maybe a *very* little," I admit, rushing on over her laughter. "What professional athlete wearing a towel hits on a journalist in the locker room? Like, who does that?"

"You said yourself it was ten years ago."

"It was humiliating, and the guys on the beat teased me about it mercilessly. It took a long time for me to live that down." I stop pacing to face Sadie, digging in my heels literally and figuratively. "Besides, he may have been a professional athlete, but he's a novice commentator. No damn way I'm working with him."

"Okay, for real, *mami*?" Sadie tips her head, setting a shiny dark curtain of hair in motion. "You are all caps right now and I need you lower case."

"Isn't there someone else?" I perch on the end of the desk and kick my foot out to tap her knee. "Work with me here."

"No, there isn't." Sadie glares at the seaweed like it's compelling her to pop another strand of it in her mouth. "And I couldn't do anything to change this if I wanted to, which I don't."

"You're the producer. Of course, you have a say."

"Not in this one. Came from the very top." Sadie catches the heel of the shoe I'm banging against my desk. "Hey. It's a coup to have Deck co-hosting. He's been doing guest spots all season, and killing it. In addition to being a basketball genius, he's articulate and willing to learn. He may be new to commentating, but he's a natural on camera."

"I know," I admit grudgingly. "I've seen him."

"So what's the problem? I never heard much about the towel thing after the initial hoopla."

"No, they ended up reassigning me, and after the initial round of teasing, it died down." I extract my shoe from her grip and walk over to the window, no less impressed by the New York City view today than when I first landed this job and this office.

"Then I don't see the problem," Sadie says from behind me.

I don't face her and maybe I don't want to face myself.

There's always been a huge question mark over MacKenzie Decker. What would have happened if I had gone against my better judgment and taken him up on his offer of "or something"? What if I hadn't been reassigned from his team's beat? All I know of him has been through the news and by reputation over the years, but every time I hear his name . . . I don't know. Something stirs in me, and I'm not sure I'm quite ready for stirring.

So much has happened for us both, I know that encounter at his locker should be water long under the bridge. Deck won an MVP, two championships, and every award that counts. He got married. Divorced. Injured. Retired. I'm helming my own show on SportsCo, one of the biggest sports networks around. I was engaged. My brain short circuits before I go any further because I can't deal with all the *feelings* today. Not about my fiancé.

"You seem on edge. Is it . . ." Sadie's voice is careful in the way I've come to hate.

"Is it Will?"

She can be irritatingly clairvoyant at times.

"I'm fine." My mouth autopilots the words, a knee-jerk response to the question people have asked me a thousand times in a thousand different ways over the last year.

"If you need to—"

"I said I'm fine, Sade." I swivel a look over my shoulder that tells her not to push. For once she listens.

"Okay. Just saying I'm here. I know things have been—" Her mother's ring tone, Ricky Martin's "Livin' la Vida Loca," interrupts. "Hold on."

Thank God for Mama and Ricky Martin. This is the last thing I want to discuss.

"What, Ma?" Sadie asks, phone pressed to her ear.

That's the last English word from her mouth for the next five minutes since Sadie unleashes a torrent of Spanish to the woman on the other line. The only words I understand are "burrito" and "Atlanta Housewives."

I'm grateful for this brief reprieve from our conversation. Bad enough I have to work with Mack Decker. Now the feelings and memories that come with Will rise up and try to steal any peace, any confidence I've found.

"Yeah, yeah," Sadie says, easing back into English. "I'll tell her."

"Tell me what?" I demand, leaning my back against the cool glass of my window.

"How do you know she meant you?" Sadie lifts one perfectly threaded brow.

"She always means me. She loves me." I shrug. "What'd Ma say?"

"She wants you to meet my cousin Geraldo."

I chortle. That's the best way to describe the amused sound I make. I cover my mouth when Sadie glares at me.

"Sorry, Sade."

"Don't hate on my cousin, Avery."

"I'm sorry." A helpless laugh belies my apology. "As a journalist, how do you expect me to take a man named Geraldo seriously? Besides, you know I have no desire to date anyone."

"I know it's hard, and maybe it's too soon for an actual relationship," Sadie says, sympathy and determination all over her face. "But just meeting someone? That's not so bad. I just . . . you have to move on. And you never talk about it."

I swallow past the guilt clogging my throat and nod quickly, dismissively. I only talk about Will to my therapist. If you aren't charging me two hundred dollars an hour, these lips are sealed.

"You know I'm here if you need me," Sadie finally speaks softly and stands, nodding when my only response is a quick auto-smile. "Wanna grab something to eat?"

"Nah." I gesture to the open laptop planted in the spill of papers on my desk. "I got another couple hours of prep for tomorrow's show."

"Speaking of which, can you come in a little early to go over things with Decker?"

"He's starting *tomorrow*?" My mouth falls open and my heart starts running like a motor. "I can go one day without a co-host. Give me a day at least to get ready."

"You've had day-of host changes before," Sadie reminds me while she sways her hips to the door. "You're a professional. What's there to get ready for?"

Even after a decade, I still recall with perfect clarity the golden-brown hair, darkened and damp from his shower, curling at the nape of his strong neck. The chiseled landscape of chest and abs. The long legs, sculpted and bronzed extending beyond the small protective square of white terry cloth. I've only seen Mack Decker a handful of times over the years at awards shows, events, and the like. Usually he was with his wife and I was with Will. We were always cordial and polite, but somewhere deep in the secret corners of my heart, I allowed myself the tiniest bit of disappointment that he remained a question all these years. Sure, for a few weeks after the towel incident I was humiliated and offended and pissed off.

And flattered.

And intrigued.

And . . . turned on.

Three things I don't have time or space in my life for right now.

"It was ten years ago, Avery," I mumble, sitting in my chair to examine analytics for tomorrow's show.

Decker has always been an unanswered question. Bottom line under all my excuses, now that the opportunity may re-present itself, maybe I'm not ready for the answer.

Chapter 3

Avery

MacKenzie Decker's arrogance is tailor-made, draped over him like one of his Armani suits. Fitted to his shoulders by years of fawning fans. Tapered to the broad, muscular back through a myriad of accolades, trophies, titles and championship rings. Perfectly fit to slide along the muscled length of his legs when he strides into SportsCo like he owns the place.

He *could* own the place. His net worth is no secret thanks to year after year on *Forbes* Highest Paid Athletes list. Most of his money comes from endorsements, not the lucrative NBA contracts he netted for twelve seasons. That smile. Those eyes. That body. His charm. Fifth Avenue served him up and Main Street feasted, making him a household name practically from the moment he was drafted.

He definitely doesn't need this job. Maybe that's what bothers me most.

He doesn't need this job. I do.

He didn't have to work to get here. I did.

Graduating at the top of my journalism class from Howard University, paying my dues on crowded sidelines, discarding modesty in locker rooms of naked men—I did whatever it took to get my own show. He just walks right in fresh from retirement like the party should start now that he's here. My show is just a pit stop between his storied career and the Hall of Fame. It grinds my teeth that he sits in the seat across from me like it's a throne. Like this is all his due and his kingdom. Like I'm his subject.

Yeah. That's what bothers me.

It better not be the way his presence sizzles in the air like hot oil tossed into a frying pan. It better not be his scent, clean and male with an undercurrent of lust. Or his amber-colored eyes surrounded by a wedge of thick lashes. It better not be any of those things because I had a talk with my body this morning, and we decided by mutual agreement that I would not respond physically to this man.

"Decker, welcome!" Sadie says, her smile unusually bright and her eyes slightly dazzled. "We're so glad to have you."

That slow-building smile starts behind his eyes, quirks his sinfully full lips and creases at the corners. We're roughly the same age. He's a little older, so he must be thirty-five, thirty-six or so by now, and the years have been oh so kind. If it hadn't been for a career-ending injury last year, he'd still be balling.

"I'm glad to be here." The voice, modulated and slightly southern, is that graveled rasp typically only earned by a few packs a day, except Decker is famously fastidious about what goes into his body, temple that it is. Nature just granted him that voice. I remind myself not to inspect all the other things nature awarded this man.

"You know Avery of course." The look Sadie turns on me holds a subtle threat in case I'm feeling froggy this morning. Lucky for her I had my cold brew coffee. That stuff keeps me out of jail. I'd hate to meet me without it.

I extend my hand, which he immediately enfolds in his. It's warm and huge. You forget how big these guys are when you watch them on television, but standing here in the well-toned flesh, Decker towers over me by at least a foot. He makes me feel small and delicate. I *love* feeling small and delicate . . . said no self-respecting sports reporter ever. Add that to the ever-growing list of things he makes me feel that I don't like.

"Good to see you again, Avery." He looks down at our hands still clasped.

"Yeah, you, too." I wiggle my fingers for him to let go, and for a moment mischief breaks through his neutral expression, before he releases me and sits at the conference room table.

"Thanks for stepping in, Deck," Sadie says. "How's the penthouse suite?"

SportsCo has a great relationship with the luxury hotel across the street, often holding events and putting up guests there. I'm assuming Deck is staying in the penthouse while he's with the show.

"It's great," Deck says. "Glad I don't have to commute from Connecticut every day."

"Well we wanted to make it easy for you. Let us know if you need anything." Sadie hands us both folders. "Now did you guys get my email with the rundown of today's show?"

When we both nod, Sadie dives into the details. I was prepared to be unimpressed. So many athletes assume because they played their sport, they know *all* sports and can just hop in front of a camera and it'll be fine. Deck obviously didn't make that assumption. He's prepared. And I've seen him commentate since he retired. He's good.

There's a studied ease to him, a carefully cloaked intensity. People can't always handle the passion it takes to do great things. I'm allergic to average and abhor mediocrity. That leaks into every aspect of my life. Type A. Driven. I'm not sure what you'd call it, but it's all over Mack Decker, too. He was renowned for it on the court, the alpha dog leading his pack to victory by any means necessary. As we review the elements of today's show, I look up more than once to find all of that intensity fixed on me. The dark gold stare pins me to my ergonomic leather seat. I make sure not to squirm, though it feels like, with nothing more than sex appeal and quiet tenacity, he's holding me hostage.

"All good?" Sadie looks between the two of us once we're done, but her query targets me. I know this because I know Sadie. I didn't want Decker stepping in, but even I can't deny his professionalism and competence. And obviously he'll be catnip for our viewers. Every excuse to *not* want him here keeps melting away. Eventually I'll have to deal with the real reason I've resisted him as a guest host.

But not yet.

"Yeah." I scribble nonsense on the pad in front of me, one of the many ways I exert my abundant nervous energy. "All sounds good to me."

Decker glances at the papers in front of him. "I'll try to keep it together in the last segment when Magic Johnson comes on set."

"What?" The word rides a laugh past my lips. "Are you serious?"

"I'm not allowed to lose my shit over the greatest point guard to ever lace up?" He leans back, lips twitching and arms crossed over the expanse of chest hidden beneath his crisp shirt.

"I'm glad you qualified *point* guard, not shooting guard, because we'd have a problem if you don't acknowledge Jordan as the Almighty Guard."

Decker's deep-timbered chuckle moves the muscles of his throat and slides over me like a lasso, roping me in and tugging me closer.

"I'm not having the Greatest of All Time debate with you, Avery."

"Good because there's no debate about who the GOAT is." I toss my pen on the table like a gauntlet. "You tell me anyone other than Jordan, we got a problem."

He expels a disdainful puff of air.

"Then we got a problem."

"Heresy." I lean forward, salivating for a good debate with a worthy opponent. "Who you got?"

He holds up three fingers. "Wilt, Kareem and Russell."

"Three!" Outrage drags the word from my mouth. "How can you have three ahead of Jordan? MJ at number four is just . . . I . . . I . . . just . . ."

"While she tries to gather her thoughts," Sadie interjects with a grin and a glance at her phone. "I gotta take this. Thanks again, Decker. Let's have a great first show."

When Sadie leaves, there's no buffer between me and the wall of fine ass-ness that is MacKenzie Decker. It's the first time we've been alone since he faced me naked in a roomful of laughing men a decade ago. I clear my throat needlessly since I have nothing to say. I felt safe with Sadie as our chaperone. Now that it's just the two of us, I can't remember what we were talking about with so much ease.

"You were saying?" Decker watches me expectantly.

"Huh?" I stall and blank-face him. "What was I saying?"

"Greatest of all time?" he prompts, anticipation brewing in his eyes.

"I'll have to school you later." I force a smile, gathering the papers in front of me, tucking them into a neat stack and pressing them to my chest. "I need to review some tape from last night's games before the show. See you on set."

I walk to the door and wave over my shoulder.

"I never got to apologize properly for the towel."

His words, injected seamlessly into our conversation, stunt my steps. We were doing just fine until he had to go *there*.

"What?" I turn to consider him warily, half-hoping he'll let it go, but there's no going back now. The polite façade has fallen away, baring his curiosity, his determined frankness.

"I said," he pauses deliberately to make sure I'm hearing him clearly this time, "I never got to apologize properly for the towel. I know there was some teasing on the circuit afterwards."

"It was a long time ago," I reply stiffly. "It's fine."

"I reached out, but I wasn't sure if—"

"I got the messages you left at the station." I keep my tone neutral and project confidence. "Thank you."

"But you never . . ." There's a trail of silence after his incomplete thought.

"I was reassigned." I shift my feet and glance into the hall beyond the conference room, signaling that I'm ready to be done with this conversation. "I knew we wouldn't see each other much, so . . ."

I leave a trail of my own, shrugging and hoping we can conclude this.

"Your hair used to be curly," he says, a grin accompanying yet another abrupt shifting of gears.

"Yes, well—"

"I liked it," he cuts in, stuttering my heartbeat and drifting a glance over my hair. "It's still beautiful this way."

He locks his whisky-tinted eyes with mine.

"You're still beautiful."

"Um, well, I—"

"We should grab a drink," he says, further disconcerting me. *"Or something."*

He drops his words from that night on me, when he wore nothing but a tiny towel and super-size bravado.

Humor and irritation war inside me at the shared memory before I get them both under control.

"Look, Deck . . ." I shake my head and trap my bottom lip in my teeth before going on. "It's still a no."

He opens his mouth as if he has more to say, but my rigid expression must convince him he really shouldn't.

"Well, glad that's all behind us." The sorcerer smile, the one he must use to put people at ease, reappears. "I'll let you go prepare. See you on set."

I nod and turn on my heel, making sure to keep my steps steady and measured, even though I want to run back to my office before he decides to press the advantage I don't want him to know he has.

Chapter 4

Decker

There's something about Avery Hughes that rubs me the right way.

She gets me worked up. It starts, as with most men, in my pants, but in no time it reaches my *other* head, the one with the brain, and it's her wit and sharp intelligence, her drive that keeps me wanting more. Even if there hadn't been all the ribbing after the towel incident, I still would have thought about her for days after we met. She's the kind of woman who makes an impression and lingers in your memory.

I last saw her about two years ago at a *Sports Illustrated* party. I'd been injured that season, and was pretty sure my NBA career was over. Even though my wife Tara stood at my side, glittering and clinging possessively, we both knew our marriage was over, too. It had been on life support for a while. We were scheduled to present a check from my charitable foundation that night, so we had to attend together, but we'd already filed the papers. Still, when I spotted Avery across the room with her fiancé, guilt chewed through my gut because I wanted to walk away from my soon-to-be-ex, snatch Avery from that dude and take her to some corner; pick up where we'd left off in that locker room.

It feels like I've lived a dozen lives since then. Seasons in the NBA should be measured like dog years. Not just the wear and tear on your body, but the wear and tear on your soul. Greedy people, shattered hopes, broken marriages.

Missed chances.

Avery feels like the biggest missed chance of all. Maybe she retained that mystery because I never got to know her. Never got to taste her. That night at the *SI* party, when our glances collided across eight years and a crowded room, I had to accept that I never would. I had only seen her a handful of times and from a distance since our first meeting, but in a moment, before she had time to disguise it, her unguarded expression told me she hadn't forgotten. That I was still . . . something, even if it was just an annoying, awkward memory. Avery, being the consummate professional, contorted her lips into a plastic smile and turned back to the man at her side.

Only that man hasn't been at her side the last few months. Lately, the few times I watched her show, the ring she wore that night was gone. I'm not sure what's happened, but the ring's not there now, and I'm assuming . . . okay, *hoping* . . . the man is gone, too.

When SportsCo called about subbing as Avery's co-host on *Twofer*, I cancelled whatever my team had lined up to make it happen. This could get interesting . . . if Avery would let it.

If she would let *me*.

We're a week in, and on camera, Avery and I have a natural connection that viewers are loving, but she's kept me at a polite distance otherwise. When the lights go down, her guard goes up, and she presents that phony, careful neutrality she thinks will keep me out. But every day, I see a new crack in that wall she hides behind, and it only stokes my curiosity to see what's in there. It's time to chip away at the wall. Time to be the hammer.

I study her during our production meeting. She's making a point to the team about a camera angle. An image of her pinned against the conference room door highjacks my imagination; my tongue plunged so deeply down her throat she'd have to beg for breath. Of me sliding to my knees and pushing that skirt past her thighs, pulling her legs onto my shoulders and roughly shoving her panties aside. Of my mouth open and worshiping between her legs. Of my face wet from her passion gushing onto me.

I mentally run through the list that usually keeps a hard-on at bay, but it's not working this time, and my dick is a pipe in my pants. I would handle this woman. I would pick her up when I kiss her. Literally sweep her off her feet and hold her by the ass. Show her what it feels like to be kissed suspended in the air. I'd press her against me so she felt how much I wanted her. Until she felt my erection and had to deal with it. Until she had to deal with *me*. I scoot my chair another inch under the table, struggling to rein in this fantasy.

If this woman is indifferent to me, I'll eat both my championship rings. I made my living reading plays and picking apart defenses. From my experience, people and relationships aren't much different, and there's no way I misread the attraction between us that badly. She's not a woman you can rush, but I only have two weeks left on my guest stint before good ol' dick pic returns. With so little time left on the clock, I think this calls for the full-court press. End-to-end coverage. Man-to-man defense . . . or in this case, man-to-woman. No letting up until the opponent is worn down. I live for this shit. No one can beat me at this game.

"Does that sound good?" Avery interrupts my inner pep talk, long-lashed eyes blinking at me over the cup of cold brew I've been bringing her every day.

What the hell are we talking about?

I glance around the conference room, packed with the crew for the production meeting. Everyone's watching me expectantly.

"Deck?" Avery asks with a tiny frown. "I said does that sound good?"

"Hmmmm . . ." I scrunch my face like I'm pondering the subject really hard, hoping she'll elaborate.

"I mean, if you want to do the Holiday predictions last instead," she continues. "We totally can."

"Nah." *Ah! The Holiday predictions. Right.* "We can leave it at the top."

She tilts her head and narrows her eyes. "You mean in the middle?"

"Middle, yeah." I nod sagely. "Perfect place for it."

"Well if we're all agreed," Sadie says, closing her laptop. "That's a wrap."

Everyone starts dispersing. I'll find some reason to linger until Avery finishes the discussion she's having with one of the show's writers.

"Don't worry," Sadie whispers to me while she finishes packing her things. "She's coming, too."

If I take my eyes off Avery for even a second, she might dart off. That woman has become really good at avoiding me. I spare Sadie a quick glance to figure out what she's even talking about.

"Coming where?" I ask. "Who?"

"You really *were* checked out." She laughs, shaking her head and shoving her phone into her purse. "Sorry if we bore you with the details of planning the show."

"It's not personal." I do an Avery check—still chatting—before looking back to Sadie. "I hate meetings. Always have, and my mind tends to drift. So, who's going where and what's up?"

"We're all going to grab drinks and dinner."

No, thanks.

"I don't think I'll—"

"And Avery's coming with us," Sadie cuts in with a knowing look.

Oh, well in that case.

"Man's gotta eat." She and I share a conspiratorial grin. "What gave me away?"

"Um, what *didn't*?" Sadie leans against the conference room table. "Bringing her coffee every day. Not leaving any room until she does. The way you—"

"All right, all right." I glance around self-consciously to see if anyone heard her spouting how whipped I've been behaving. "So, what do I do about it, since you know so much?"

"*Do* about it?" Her smile is just relishing the novel positon I'm in having to chase a woman.

"I didn't think I'd ever have a shot. She was wearing some other guy's ring the last time I saw her. I don't want to waste my chance this time."

The humor on Sadie's face fades, her eyes go sober.

"Oh, Deck. You don't know."

"Don't know what?"

Before she can enlighten me, Avery walks up and Sadie's mouth snaps shut and her eyes stretch with some silent warning I'm clueless about.

"What's with all the lollygagging?" Avery asks, playfully bumping Sadie's shoulder, her mouth stretched into a wide grin. "We eating or what?"

I wish she'd be that easygoing with me. Despite our chemistry onscreen, I can barely get her alone long enough to have a decent conversation.

"I was just telling our friend here he should come with us." Sadie smiles up at me. "Right, Deck?"

Avery's grin slips, but she recovers quickly enough to offer me a polite, if stiff, smile.

"You should," she tells me. "This place does a great dirty martini, and I love their steak."

I rarely drink and gave up red meat years ago.

"Two of my favorite things," I lie. "What are we waiting for?"

The prospect of a few extra hours to crack her tough outer shell has my blood humming through my veins like it's pre-game and I'm facing an especially challenging opponent.

We're all crowded in the elevator on our way down, and I meet the guarded interest in Avery's eyes I've become accustomed to over the last week. Not an opponent. I think we're on the same team. I think we want the same thing. She just doesn't know it yet.

Chapter 5

Avery

Two of his favorite things, my ass.

Decker ignored the steaks, went straight for the pan roasted sea bass, and has been drinking water all night.

I take a long, grateful sip of my second martini, thanking God for whomever had the foresight to invent them. It's a massage, a hot bath and an orgasm all shaken and stirred into one delightfully numbing concoction. And the closer we get to Christmas, the more numb I need to be.

"You look like you're enjoying that," Decker says, pushing his plate away.

"And it looks like you *didn't* enjoy that." I nod toward his half-eaten fish.

"No, it was delicious. I just wasn't as hungry as I thought I was."

"And you decided to forego the alcohol, too? Even though martinis and steak are your faves?"

I shouldn't toy with him, but it's kind of fun watching a man so notoriously pursued by women making excuses to spend time with *me*, even though I'm not exactly sure what he wants.

Scratch that.

The barely concealed lust steaming in his eyes tells me what he wants. Problem is, I think I might want it, too, but I can't. If my vagina was the only thing I had to worry about, this would be a no-brainer. Six feet and seven inches of tanned, beautiful *man*. What's there to think about? But even just in our first week working together, I've seen a depth to him I didn't expect. The same determination and commitment to excellence that has him Hall of Fame-bound, he's applied to guest hosting. TV's a steep learning curve, and I gotta give it to him. He's doing a great job. He's funny, sharp, thinks on his feet, and can talk any other sport almost as easily as he can basketball. For most women that wouldn't be a turn on, but for me?

Yeah, very much so.

With a man like Decker, the vajayjay isn't the only body part to consider. He could endanger my heart, and that troubled organ still hasn't recovered from Will.

"So, seems like we have pretty much opposite picks for every prediction," Decker says, leaning back in his seat.

"Prediction?" I snap out of my own thoughts and tune into our conversation. "What do you mean?"

"For the Holiday Picks segment." Decker lifts his brows, waiting for me to catch up. "For next week's show."

"Oh, yes," I deadpan, warming to a subject I'm comfortable discussing. "Shocking that we're at odds."

"I know, right?" He leans forward to rest his elbows on the table and turns his body toward me, effectively blocking out the rest of the table. "We both have the Wolves and the Sabers going to the NCAA Championship, but I have the Wolves winning. You picked the Sabers."

"Yeah, because Caleb Bradley and the Sabers took it last year," I remind him. "What makes you think they won't do it again?"

"August West makes me think they won't do it again. If West hadn't sprained his ankle last year, he could have taken it then. He's got that killer instinct."

"If we're both right and they both advance, it'll be one helluva final no matter who comes out on top."

"It'll be West. Mark my words. I recognize a champ in the making when I see one. Caleb Bradley may be the All-American Golden Boy, but August is the one to watch."

His smile is smug, but I can't help smiling in return. It's basketball. I know my shit, but he's *lived* it and has two championships to show for the years he put into the League.

"Who am I to disagree? You *are* the future Hall of Famer." My sarcasm delivers the compliment backhanded.

"Don't you forget it," he replies with a chuckle.

"Did you always know you wanted to play ball?" I shock myself by asking. I don't do lengthy conversations with this man. Or at least I haven't over the last week. This martini must be dirtier than I thought. It's going to my head. As long as it doesn't start heading south, we should be okay.

"Always." He shrugs. "Honestly it could have gone either way. Basketball or football. I had looks for both."

"You were scouted for both sports? College?"

"Yeah, I played both even through high school, but it came to the point I had to choose."

"What position did you play? Football, I mean, obviously." Everyone knows he's one of the greatest point guards to ever play basketball.

"What do you think I played?" He props his chin in his hand, the bourbon-flavored eyes brimming with curiosity. About me.

"Hmmm." I tip my head and squint one eye, assessing. "Your leadership skills are off the chart."

"Well, thank you." He dips his head and smiles to acknowledge the compliment.

"You don't follow others well."

His smile falters, and he glares at me, even though there's still humor in his eyes.

"You always think you know best," I continue, enjoying this more by the second. "And you love ordering people around."

"Okay, maybe I should just tell you before you really hurt my feelings."

"Like I could," I scoff.

He doesn't answer, but looks down at the table, a smile curling the corners of his wide, sensual mouth.

"Quarterback," I say triumphantly. "Am I right?"

His laugh is richer than the chocolate ganache I ordered, but shouldn't eat.

"God, I wish I could say you're wrong," he admits with a grin. "Yeah, quarterback."

"I knew it." I brush my shoulders off.

"Uh huh. Now who's the know it all?"

"Oh, I don't deny it." I take a sip of my neglected drink. "I always assume I have the right answer."

"I have observed that over the last week." He shoots me a speculative glance before continuing. "There's a lot I haven't learned, though."

The vodka seems to pause midway down my throat. I cough a little and wait for him to start the questions I've seen in his eyes for days.

"Like did you play any sports yourself?" he asks.

I breathe a little easier. This is comfortable territory.

"Track and field."

"Ahhh." He nods as if answering himself. "That explains it."

"Explains what?" I ask, taking another sip.

His eyes burn a trail over my neck and breasts until the table interrupts his view.

"Your body."

I cough again, reaching for a napkin to wipe my mouth.

"My-my body?" I hate how breathy I sound all of a sudden. With a few well-placed words and a look, he has me sputtering and simmering.

"I'm sure you know women who run track and field often develop a certain body type," he says, leaning forward until I can't see much of anything beyond the width of his shoulders. "Lean arms."

Even though my arms are hidden beneath my blouse, my skin heats up when he runs his eyes over them.

"Muscular legs," he continues, locking his eyes with mine. "A tight, round—"

"I'm aware," I cut in, "of what my body looks like. I see it every day."

"Wish I could say the same."

My face heats up. I know a blush doesn't show through my complexion, but judging by the way his grin goes wider and wickeder, it doesn't take color in my cheeks to tell him I'm heating up.

"So, you chose basketball." I shift the conversation back to safer ground that won't burn under my feet like hot coals.

"Yes." His grin lingers, but he indulges my redirection. "All through college."

"And then the NBA," I add.

"Yeah, if you work hard as hell and sacrifice just about everything else in your life, dreams really do come true." He grimaces. "At least some of them do."

I heard about his divorce, but don't want to assume that's what he means. He glances up, a wry twist to his lips.

"You wear your questions all over your face, Avery."

I huff a short laugh. "Do I?"

"I did have a dream other than basketball, if you're curious." His shoulders lift and fall, but they seem to be lifting more weight than he lets on. "I wanted a wife, kids, the whole package."

"And you got them, right?" I ask softly.

I want to ask what went wrong. I wonder if that question is on my face, too, because he answers without me voicing it.

"Tara, my ex, and I didn't as much grow apart, as we never should have been together."

I've thought that of Will and me many times. Wondered if things would have ended differently if he'd never met me. Sometimes it keeps me up at night. Sometimes it's the first thing I think about when I wake up.

"Statistically, half of all married couples would say the same thing." I smile my sympathy. "And kids? I heard you had a daughter."

"Yeah, my little girl Kiera." The rugged lines of his face noticeably soften. "You wanna see?"

I nod, surprisingly eager to see how his DNA played out on a little female face.

"Oh, she's so pretty, Deck," I whisper, my eyes glued to his phone screen. She's blonde and looks uncannily like the woman I saw Decker with at a *Sports Illustrated* party a couple of years ago. Her eyes, though, are golden brown, just like her father's. I glance up from the phone.

"She has your eyes."

"That's about it." He chuckles, accepting his phone and glancing affectionately at the picture before setting it on the table. "I can't take much credit for how beautiful she is."

I look away, afraid my eyes would betray my thoughts as clearly as he said he could see them. Afraid he'll see that I think he's the most beautiful specimen I've ever encountered. That sometimes during the show, I almost lose my train of thought wondering how his tawny hair would feel wrapped around my fingers. That in just a week, I've memorized the curve of his mouth and how he smells. Not his cologne, but that rawer scent made from nothing but skin and bone and him that rests just below the veneer of civilization we all wear.

"Tara just moved to LA," Decker continues, a rueful set to his lips. "And took Kiera with her."

"I'm sorry." I frown. "It must be harder to see her now with you still on the East Coast, I guess?"

"Yeah. Takes a little more work, but she's worth it. I've accomplished a lot, but she's the best thing I've ever done." He shrugs and then turns an inquisitive look on me. "What about you?"

"What about me?" My fingers tighten around the fragile stem of my martini glass. My heart tightens in my chest, braced for questions I'll have to evade.

"Well, I know you were engaged," he says with a careful look at my bare ring finger. "And I don't think you are anymore."

He doesn't know.

I savor that tiny slice of time while I can where he doesn't know.

For the last year of my life, everyone has known what happened. And I often feel smothered under the weight of their speculation, their awkward sympathy, their damn good intentions because they know everything. Well, they *think* they know everything. I have my secrets; secrets kept alive only by me because only Will knew.

And now Will is gone.

"He died." I clear my throat, my lips trembling in the most vexing way. I steady them like I've learned to steady my emotions. "Will, my fiancé, died last year around this time actually."

When I say *everyone* knows, it's not like when "everyone" knows Deck got a divorce or the details of a multimillion-dollar contract he inked. When "everyone" knows what's going on in his life, it's the world. His fame is much broader than mine. I'm a sportscaster, and I'm on television, but my life isn't national news, much less international. With Deck, the whole world could know his business. The whole world doesn't know my fiancé died last December. Only everyone who knows me and everyone who knew Will. Everyone in my life knows. And now so does Decker.

For the last few minutes, it was easy to forget that just beyond the barrier of Deck's torso and shoulders, our colleagues are drinking and talking. Laughing and blowing off steam after a long day. I didn't realize how completely Deck had managed to isolate us; to monopolize me until it gets so quiet in our little corner.

"Avery, I'm so sorry." His voice is a soft rumble of compassion. "I had no idea. I hadn't heard."

I nod, panicking as a familiar knot ignites inside my throat, threatening to choke me. Out of habit and necessity, I start blinking rapidly against ill-timed tears.

"Yeah, it wasn't . . . something we broadcast." Dark humor taunts the corner of my mouth. "Will would have hated that; to be a part of some media circus. He wasn't . . . he was the last one to draw attention to himself."

A door cracks open that I keep closed and locked; that I try to forget exists. The one with all my memories of Will. His smile, which had become so rare at the end. It was the first thing I liked about him; that his smile was kind and genuine. I can't do this. Not here. Not now. Not with Decker watching my face for signs of distress. If he keeps looking, he'll find it. It's not as deeply buried as I manage to convince most people. Decker isn't most people, and I instinctively know he won't be fooled.

"It's getting late." My smile is a cold, waxy curve trying its best to look alive. "I think I'll go."

"Avery," he says softly. Just that. Just my name, but there's so much more there, and I can't do this shit right now.

I ignore him and reach down to grab my purse, using those few seconds to compose myself and swipe at the corners of my eyes. When I stand, so does he. Our eyes clash for a moment, mine watery and his concerned. I step around him, snapping the thread strung taut between us, and address my coworkers.

"Okay, guys." I spread a bright smile around to everyone. "I'm heading out. Have a good weekend."

Blindly, I make my way to the door, longing for the fresh air, at least as fresh as New York City has to offer.

"Hey, Ave," Sadie calls from behind me when I'm just a few feet away from the exit. "Wait up."

I stop and turn, smoothing my expression into patient inquiry, hoping the churning waves in my gut aren't washing up on my face.

"You okay?" Sadie sees more than most. She knows more than most, too, but even she doesn't know everything.

"I'm fine." I roll my eyes when she gives me the look that says *it's me you're talking to*. "Okay. I'm not exactly fine, but I will be."

"Do you need—"

"I just need to go home, Sade." There's a pleading note in my voice that I can't suppress much longer. "Please. Just let me get out of here."

Sadie nods, hooks her arm around my neck and whispers into my ear.

"It's gonna get better, babe."

Some things don't. Some things never get better because they can never be undone. I had to learn that for myself the hardest way. I won't try to teach Sadie at the hostess stand of this nice restaurant.

"Night," I settle for saying before walking swiftly to the door.

I draw in great lungfuls of the cold night air and start walking. With every step, my heart decelerates and my breath evens and my tears dry up. That's all I needed. Some time to myself.

"Avery!" a deep voice calls from behind me.

So much for time to myself.

I turn to find Decker almost caught up to me, his long legs making quick work of the few feet separating us. I wanted to be alone, and he's ruining that. Yet my heart lifts a little at the sight of him. I knew it! If my vagina and my heart ever get on the same page, they'll be my downfall.

"Can you not take a hint?" My voice lacks the irritation it should hold.

"Only the ones I want to take," he replies easily, hunching into his dark coat and squinting against the cold. "You walking?"

"Obviously since you're walking to catch me."

"Ahhh." He grins, slanting me an amused look. "The smartass is back."

My answering smile dims as I remember what chased me out of the restaurant in the first place.

"I meant are you walking all the way home?" he asks.

"It's not far." I glance up at him. "And I don't need an escort."

"Well you got one, lady."

I roll my eyes, which only makes him laugh. We're silent for the next few steps, and I focus on the bustling anonymity of the city. You can get lost in this hectic, harried press of humanity. I have over the last year. I've hidden myself in its crevices and I've hurt in my solitude. I thought it was what I deserved—to hurt alone. With Decker here, the sounds of the city swallowing up the yawning silence inside of me, I wonder if maybe I've been wrong. It feels good to have someone . . . here. Just here. Not demanding answers, or hovering for fear I'll self-destruct. But someone who just wants my company and wants to offer theirs. It dents my loneliness.

"Here I am." I stop in front of my apartment building and turn to Deck, prepared to say good-bye.

Of course, he walks ahead to the entrance. My doorman recognizes him instantly, rushing over to hold the glass doors wider for him.

"Deck, we sure miss seeing you on the court," he says, an eager grin splitting his face.

"Can't say I miss being out there as much as I thought I would," Decker replies, signing the slip of whatever paper the doorman found for his autograph. "I like not aching and creaking half the year. Eighty-two games for twelve years will kick your ass."

"Not to mention playoffs in the post-season," the doorman reminds him with an admiring grin.

"Yeah, there were a few of those, too, huh?" Decker laughs and turns when the elevator arrives. "Nice meeting you."

"Great meeting you, too. Thanks for the autograph. My son'll love this. Good night, Ms. Hughes," the doorman adds, finally acknowledging me.

I return his smile, not minding being ignored. It's not every day you see a living sports legend. I remember feeling that way the first night I met Decker, even though I still had to ask him tough questions. He'd won rookie of the year the season before and was already one of the brightest stars in the League. Remembering the towel incident makes me smile as we get off the elevator.

"What are you grinning about?" Deck asks, narrowing his eyes in false suspicion. "I don't trust you when you grin like that."

Feeling a little lighter, I turn to face him, walking backward toward my door.

"I was thinking about the first night we met."

"Ugh." He shakes his head and closes his eyes briefly. "I was such an immature asshole."

"I think I told you that then." I laugh when he glowers at me. "You just admitted it. I'm agreeing with you. Be happy."

"You know it's funny. That was ten years ago." His smile as we keep walking borders on wistful, if such firm lips could be described that way. "So it feels like I've known you forever, but before I started the show last week, we'd never had a real conversation. I mean, unless you count the one at my locker."

"I don't." I lean against the door to my apartment. "You were wearing a towel, and not even that at one point."

"Nice." He stops in front of me. "I'll never live that down with you, will I?"

"Do you really want to?"

"Nope," he admits with a shameless, cocksure grin. "At least I knew you would never forget me."

As if I could.

I don't say the words, but something on my face must confess that I never forgot him. That sometimes in quiet moments alone, he was always an unanswered question. Or maybe I was afraid to ask. His humor evaporates, and his eyes take on that fierce focus I'd always noted when I watched him play. The camera would catch this exact look on his face; like the prize is in sight, and it was only a matter of four quarters before his opponent would yield. I wonder which quarter we're in.

"So, like I was saying." He picks up where he left off, that intense stare like steam hovering over my skin. "I feel like I've learned a lot about you since I started with the show."

"Is that right?" I press my shoulders into the door for support because that look is melting my bones, and I need to stand my ground.

"I know that as soon as you walk into a room, you charge the air," he says softly. "Everything comes to attention around you."

My breath stutters and I lick dry lips.

"I know that people enjoy following you so much they don't even realize you're leading them," he continues, taking a step closer and stealing another ounce of air from my lungs. "And that you're usually the smartest person in the room, but you know when to let other people think they are."

I thought butterflies in your stomach were some urban myth from Harlequin romance novels, but sure enough, something is fluttering in my belly at his words.

Aw, crap. I don't do butter fucking flies.

"And I know that as much as you light up onscreen, there's something sad in your eyes, and I hate it." He steps as close as he can, cups my cheek, locking our eyes. "I saw it tonight and I hate it, Avery."

He flattens his other hand against the door, his arms making an intimate alcove I couldn't escape if I wanted to.

I don't want to.

He pulls back just enough to search my face. Surely he sees my bottom lip trapped between my teeth because I must resist yielding to the warm comfort of him.

"I want to make it better, Ave," he whispers, the cool mint of his breath breezing over my lips. "I just want to . . ."

He scans my face, waiting for some sign from me that it's okay. That the desire to kiss me so clearly telegraphed in his eyes is okay. I can't find words to articulate that in this maelstrom of grief and desire and confusion, the only thing clear, the only thing that makes any sense right now, is for him to kiss me. So I don't say a word. I just lean forward until our lips meet.

Chapter 6

Decker

Soft and fresh like petals.

I'm a jock. Not a dumb one, but a jock nonetheless. I don't describe a woman's lips as soft and fresh or compare a kiss to flowers. Besides the few years I was married to Tara, if it opened its legs and said yes or please, I fucked it. I always rushed it. A man's got needs, but I got in and I got out. This woman, this kiss, I have to savor. I'd be a fool not to. It's a first kiss. I understand the difference now between the first time you kiss someone, and a *first kiss*. This is a discovery of tongues and lips and heat. An introduction of our souls, if that doesn't sound too pussy-ish. It's how I feel, though. Like as our lips brush back and forth, as our tongues tangle, as I taste her, mouthful by delicious mouthful, I'm learning her secrets. I'm telling her mine. My hand slides from the door to flatten into the warmth of her back through the silk blouse, bringing her incrementally closer. The air shifts and takes the shape of lust; assumes the form of want. The sound of her moaning, the slight lift and fall of her breasts against my chest, testifies that she feels it, too.

The elevator dings, and our bodies go still even as we keep exchanging breaths and heartbeats through our clothes; even though my mouth is still poised above hers. I have her against the door, and every curve of her body is impressing itself on me, making sure I'll never forget how right we fit together. I look over my shoulder toward the elevator. The doors open, but no one gets off. That interruption was enough to bring her back to her senses, though. God knows I can't find mine.

"Um . . . you should go," she whispers, a muscle rippling along the smooth line of her jaw.

I bend to breathe over her mouth, so she can taste our kisses lingering on my lips. "Or you could invite me in."

Her scent and the warmth of her body take my senses hostage. I smell her and want to kiss her again so badly it stings my taste buds. Her eyes already regret the last few moments I thought were so perfect. I can't calm my emotions or my body that quickly.

"You don't want to come in, Deck."

"I assure you I do," I tell her.

A short laugh, deceptively light, breezes past her lips. She glances down to the floor and shakes her head.

"I'd make the worst one-night stand ever," she says.

"One-night stand?" I take her chin in hand and lift, forcing her to look at me. "I've waited a long time for this path to be clear. No conflict of interest. No other people standing in our way. I don't know exactly what I want, Avery, but it's damn sure more than one night."

If anything, my assurance that it's more than just physical, more than just a night to me, lights panic in her eyes.

"Oh, that's worse." She frowns even as she sends a sad smile up at me. "I'm not anywhere near ready for something like that, Deck."

She's not a tall woman, though the strength of her personality makes you forget that. I've easily got a foot or more and a hundred pounds on her. She tucks a shiny chunk of dark hair behind her shoulder, exposing the intricate whorl of her ear, the fine angle of her jaw. She acts tough. Hell, she *is* tough, but her fiancé died only a year ago. That would leave anyone kind of fragile. Of course, she's not ready. Up this close, invading her space, past the outer wall, I see the vulnerability; the desolation and pain. It stabs me in the chest.

"I get that," I say, my voice rough. "I'm so sorry about him, Ave. About your fiancé."

She nods, the tumult churning inside evident on her face. The need to comfort her has my hand up, palming her cheek and my other hand at her waist, pulling her into me. After a hesitation, she surrenders to it. Her forehead drops to my chest, and a ragged breath shudders through her slim body. The air thickens with lingering grief. She doesn't cry, but the dip of her shoulders, the tension of her body, broadcasts how difficult this still is. My hand traces a soothing path from between her shoulders to the small of her back, and I don't say anything, but leave her to take any comfort she can from the human contact. After a few moments, she shifts.

"Thanks, Deck," she says softly, pulling back. My hand tightens at her waist, anchoring her to me, despite the gap between our bodies. She feels so good, I'm not ready to relinquish her.

"I need to go." She stares at the button on my shirt instead of at me.

I'm about to refuse; to press the issue of the connection I know she feels, too, but there is just enough shadow in her dark eyes; trace amounts of the grief that brought us into each other's arms in the first place, to change my mind. My hand drops, and she turns to unlock her apartment door.

"I'll see you on set Monday." Her eyes meet mine cautiously like she thinks I might grab her.

That could happen.

"Sure." I step back. "Should be a great show."

Once she's safely inside, I board the elevator. She's right. Tonight wasn't the night. Based on what I learned about her fiancé, I can respect that. But after tasting her, not just her sweetness, but her tears, I know this is just clemency. She wants time. I can give her space, but I'm not giving up.

Chapter 7

Avery

*H*ave yourself a merry little Christmas
Let your heart be light
From now on your troubles will be out of sight
    I wake up with Will's favorite Christmas song in my head and my hand between my legs.

Sad and horny. That's what I am. I literally cannot remember the last time I had sex. I know it was with Will because I never cheated on him in the years we were together, but our sex life was so sporadic at the end, I can't recall the last time we made love. I need to get drunk and I need to get laid. I'm hoping at least one of those will happen tonight at the SportsCo Christmas party, but it probably won't be the latter. I told Decker the truth. I'd be an awful one-night stand, and if I were in the market for one, it wouldn't be at my office Christmas party. I've never dated colleagues or athletes, and that's pretty much the extent of tonight's guest list. Will was into advertising. He could barely tell a touchdown from a homerun. I liked that he had nothing to do with sports or my career. I needed something separate from the frenetic pace of television and the crazy news cycle I'm always enslaved to.

"God, Will." I stare up at the ceiling, fresh, hot tears rolling into my ears and soaking my hairline. "Why did you do it? *How* could you do it?"

I told Decker last night that Will died, but I didn't tell him it was at his own hand.

I've been through grief counseling. I see my therapist every week. I've read about suicide and depression and know all the statistics. Seventy-five percent of suicides are men. Statistically they follow through on their attempts at higher rates. Those stats spike during the holidays. All the signs were there, but I missed them. Ignored them? Denied them? I don't know how I lived with this man and wore his ring for two years, but never knew this morbid wish was growing inside of him, a dark bud I didn't even know had taken root.

And every morning for the last year, I woke up with one question on my lips.

Why?

"The last year," I repeat, my voice an early morning croak. "Oh, my God."

He's been gone a year today. I can't believe it, and in many ways, I feel as lost as I did the night he died.

There's a call I need to make. One I dread, but know I cannot avoid.

When it rings and rolls into voice mail, I hesitate. I could call back later, but I'm not sure I can handle it today, hearing the pain in his mother's voice. I'm ashamed to feel relief that Mrs. Hattfield doesn't answer. Even more ashamed that I take the coward's way out and leave a message.

"Hi, Mrs. H," I say after the beep. "It's me, Avery."

I pause, the right words eluding me while I squeeze the cell phone like it's the only thing anchoring me.

"I . . . um . . . I know today is difficult for you." I shove the words that feel so trite out of my mouth. "It's difficult for me, too. I can't imagine . . . I just . . ."

My voice evaporates for a moment.

"I miss him," I whisper, biting my lips against a sob and

pressing my eyes closed to hold onto the last image I have of him. The deathly peace he'd taken for himself.

And it's true. I miss the guy I knew before; the one who went down on one knee at dinner and promised me forever. I even miss the sullen man who lived in the shadows the last part of his life. I'd take Will any way I could get him just to look in his eyes, grab his hands and beg him not to do it. For me. For his mother. For *himself*, to reconsider living.

"I hope you're not alone today." I take a second to compose myself before going on. "I know the next few weeks will be hard, Christmas will be hard without him."

I run one hand through my hair, frustrated that I don't have the right words and have nothing more to say.

"Okay, well, call me when you get this message," I say into the mechanical silence. "Talk to you soon."

Losing a child, it's the worst thing. When a child chooses to forfeit the very life you gave him, the pain must weigh even more. I wonder if she stares up at the ceiling some mornings asking *why* the way I do. Do her pain and grief cohabitate with a stewing rage? Does she want to drag him from the grave and shake him and call him a coward? I hate even thinking these things, but not acknowledging them to myself and at least to my therapist was ruining me. I don't know if these thoughts make me a bad person, but I know they make me sad. And frustrated. And helpless.

In my closet, I consider the row of beautiful dresses I could wear tonight. The last thing I want to do is go to a Christmas party, much less one Mack Decker is attending. Those moments at my door two weeks ago have been a source of torture. It wasn't just a reminder to my body what it's been missing, but to my emotions. That just beyond my comfort zone there may be solace for, not just my body, but for my soul.

What was I thinking? Letting him hold me? Letting him see my vulnerability? Those moments of letting go, resting against the solidity of him; being comforted by his heart beating just beyond the wall of his chest, were some of the sweetest I've had in a year. It was intoxicating, and I have no intention of getting drunk on him.

He'd go straight to my head. Straight to my heart and between my legs, and I'm not ready for any of that.

I press my thighs together against a tide of want when I recall the moments that simmered between us. Waking up thinking about Will, and getting wet knowing I'll see Deck in a few hours—it feels so wrong, but at least I'm feeling. I haven't allowed myself to want a man since Will died. Maybe no one appealed to me the way Decker does, but he's the first one to punch holes in the fence around me.

I return to my selections for the party. I've worn the black dress to several office functions. It's flattering and conservative. It's the classic "little black dress" that goes everywhere and can serve many purposes. I touch the silky material of my other option. It's a dress made of sunsets, a glorious blend of gold and red, and it still bears the tags. I've never worn it. The deep V neckline is outdone by the deeper V that bares my back. The bottom is narrow and tight and will be a testament of all the squats I've done, though my ass is mostly genetics and years of track and field. My mother and aunts have never done squats a day in their lives, and you could bounce a quarter off their butts. As good as I know the dress will look, I'm still not sure I'll wear it. It's a statement dress, and knowing Decker will be there tonight, I'm not quite sure what I want to say.

Chapter 8

Decker

"So what's next?"

The question catches me a little off guard. With a Jack and Coke halfway to my mouth, I pause to study Mike Dunlov, one of SportsCo's most popular anchors.

"I mean now that your co-hosting gig's up," he clarifies.

"Little bit of this," I answer flatly because I'm giving this guy nothing. "Little bit of that."

I toss back a portion of the much-needed drink. Playing pro ball allowed me to indulge many vices. I've had more pussy than any man has a right to in one lifetime, for example. I'm practically abstemious, though, when it comes to alcohol and what I eat. Always have been. This body was my lottery ticket, and I took care of it. But tonight, this liquor is a lifeline. It's been a bitch of a day. Mainly because my ex is being a bitch. Bad enough she moved my daughter across the country. Now she's making it harder for me to see her this Christmas. Changing my holiday plans because she's still playing the same bullshit games she did when we were married had me almost skipping this party tonight. Except . . . I watch the main entrance to see if Avery has arrived yet.

"Guy like you can write your own ticket," Mike continues. "I mean look at how you scored this hosting gig. How'd you enjoy working with Avery, by the way?"

His eyebrows waggle suggestively. "She's something else, huh?"

I stiffen, not much liking him or the look in his eyes.

"What do you mean?" I take my time sipping a little more of my drink, watching him over the glass.

"I mean, did you get any? We've all tried." He offers a careless shrug. "Who wouldn't try with a rack like that, but she was devoted to her fiancé. With him gone, she's been shut down. I just thought if anyone could finally tap that, it'd be you."

My teeth clench around an expletive. I know for a fact *Twofer* blows this douche's ratings out of the water. The respect of her colleagues is so important to Avery. Hearing him demean her this way sets me on edge.

"You're an asshole, you know that?" I ask, my tone deceptively calm, though my hand clamps around the glass while I imagine his little windpipe crushing under my fingers.

"So I've been told." He flashes his very-white veneers in that fake smile unsuspecting viewers fall for. "But there's no disrespect. It *has* been a year, and you know what the final stage of grief is, right?"

"Acceptance?"

"Nope." He leers over his scotch. "Horny. Somebody's gotta offer her a dick to cry on."

I'm two seconds from smashing my glass into his skull when his eyes latch onto something over my shoulder and light up.

"Damn," he mutters. "I really hope we've reached the final stage."

He's walking off before I process what he means, but it doesn't take long to figure out. Across the room, he and several other anchors and network executives are buzzing around Avery like she's a honeycomb. And I can't blame them. Her hair is pulled up, tendrils of it licking around her neck and ears. Simple gold earrings dangle and frame the curve of her cheekbones. Her makeup is dramatic, but simple, letting her sharply-drawn features speak for themselves. The slick of gold on her lips glimmers against the light copper of her skin.

And that dress.

This dress has to be inspiring erections all over the room. I can only speak for mine with any confidence, but it's pushing painfully against the flap of my suit pants.

The color, like saffron sprinkled over her firm curves, sets off her dusky complexion perfectly. Sleeveless, the dress showcases the feminine sculpture of her arms, and the neckline dips almost to her waist, the cut of it serving her breasts up beautifully. The bodice flows into a narrow skirt that paints the dress onto the flare of her hips and the tight line of her thighs. When she turns around and walks to the bar, many eyes zero in on her departure. The dress has no back, displaying a stretch of unblemished skin from neck to waist. The skirt strains across the high arc of her ass, and my fingers itch to squeeze it while I piston in and out, anchoring us together with nothing but my hands and my dick.

I take another measured sip, checking myself and allowing the smooth liquid to cool me off. I sound as bad as the other lechers in here. Mike may joke about her grief, but I've seen it up close. Even while the air sizzled with lust around us at her front door, I couldn't ignore the sadness in Avery's eyes. I won't take advantage of that. If I can help it, none of these horny sons of bitches will either.

"We do have hors d'oeuvres, you know," Sadie says from beside me. "You don't have to eat Avery."

I smile to acknowledge Sadie's comment and her presence, but I don't take my eyes off the only woman I'm interested in.

"I've seen the food." I glance down at Avery's best friend. "Far less appetizing than she is."

"You do always look at her like she's dessert." Sadie giggles. She's not usually a giggling kind of woman, so I attribute that tinkly sound to the glass of champagne. Probably not her first.

"I don't look at Avery like she's dessert." I drop the smile so she knows my intentions aren't of the short-lived, guilty pleasure variety. "I look at her like she's the main course."

That penetrates her tipsy bubble enough to widen her eyes with surprise.

"Hmmm." She takes another sip, brows up. "Tread carefully, if that's the case. You'd be better off settling for dessert, Deck. Short and sweet."

"Do I seem like a man who settles to you?" My laugh is humorless because I'm afraid this time I might have to.

"Avery's been through a lot this year." Sadie's eyes appear suddenly slightly sober. "And she doesn't need some player making things more complicated than they already are for her."

"*Former* player," I say. "In every sense of the word."

"Would your ex-wife agree on the former?"

"What the hell does that mean?" We trade glares over her presumption.

"Meaning I know they don't take the trash out of those tunnels every night, and ballers like you scoop it up, take it home, fuck it, and don't let a wedding ring stop you."

"I never cheated on my wife." I check the anger and frustration her assumptions are burning under my collar. "If you're asking if I got ass when I was single, then let me assure you, I got ass. If you're asking if I *still* get ass, then yeah. I *still* get ass, but if I'm in a monogamous relationship, I play one-on-one. Not that it's any of your damn business."

"Avery is my damn business." She mutters under her breath what sounds like "*cabron.*"

"If you're gonna call me a motherfucker, you can do it in English." Humor relaxes my shoulders a little after the last few tense moments.

"You speak Spanish?" She doesn't look chagrined at getting caught.

"Only enough to realize I'm being insulted from time to time."

Her mouth loosens into a slight grin before she looks up at me frankly.

"Look, Avery may seem like she's having a great time." She waves her hand at the dance floor where Avery is dancing her ass off while managing to hold a Cosmopolitan. "But like the song says, blame it on the alcohol. The last thing she needs is some one-night stand holiday cheer."

"I know that." I hate the defensive note in my voice, but I resent her thinking I'm like Mike Dunlov, looking to capitalize on Avery's vulnerability.

"But do you know that today is the day?" Sadie asks softly. "That her fiancé died a year ago today?"

"Shit." I swipe a hand over my face. "I didn't know that."

I return the assessing look Sadie's giving me, and then some. Can I trust her? Can she trust me?

"What can you tell me about him?" I ask. "About his death?"

"Nothing." Sadie's mouth tips in a wry grin. "If you're serious about Avery being the . . . how'd you put it? Main course? Then that's a story she needs to tell you herself."

"Sadie!" Jerry, a cameraman I've seen on set, calls from a few feet away. "Get out here and shake what your mama gave you."

"This may take a while." Sadie laughs and hands me her glass. "'Cause Mama gave me a lot!"

She shuffles off toward the dance floor. As soon as a server passes by, I set her glass and my barely-touched Jack and Coke on the tray. The party is in full swing, but I'm already thinking about the bed upstairs in my borrowed penthouse suite. Knowing how hard today has to be for Avery, there's no way I'm leaving her at the mercy of these wolves.

Some Mariah Carey Christmas song comes on. The one from *Love Actually*. Everyone starts singing along and dancing even harder. I hate dancing. I was that guy sitting in VIP balancing a girl on each leg since I didn't really drink and definitely didn't dance. Just posted up, which is all I plan to do tonight, too. Besides, the wall gives me a great vantage point to keep an eye on Avery. If the final stage of grief is horny, I may have to protect her from herself. With Sadie off shaking what her mama gave her, it's up to me to keep Avery's virtue intact. Ironic since I've wanted in those pants for a very long time.

Another Mariah Carey Christmas song comes on.

What is *up* with Mariah Carey and the holidays?

Some other guy steps in to dance with Avery. She's good, her body moving gracefully, that dress hanging on to her curves by a literal thread. If she pops it one more inch, I think we'll have a wardrobe malfunction on our hands. Her expression is open and free like I've never seen it, but that could be because of the drink in her hand every time she dances by.

A slower song comes on, and the guy pulls Avery close, his hands slipping to her hips and his palms drifting lower. She laughs up at him and steps back, shaking her empty glass and heading to the bar.

My turn.

"Merry Christmas." I lean against the bar and block Avery's view of the rest of the room.

The smile she's been wearing since she walked through the door wavers. Her lashes drop before she looks back up at me, that fraudulent grin firmly back in place. We've seen each other on set and in meetings, but since that kiss, I've given her the space she requested.

"Not quite Christmas." She sips the drink the bartender just handed her. "Another few days."

I glance from the alcohol to her dark, glassy eyes that, up this close, are rimmed with sorrow. "What you drinking?"

"A lot." Her laugh comes loud and hollow. "I'm drinking a lot."

"I can see that." I clear my throat and lean a little closer. "You might want to ease up. Some of these guys are on the prowl tonight."

"*They're* on the prowl?" The hazy eyes turn defiant. "Maybe *I'm* on the prowl, Deck. Maybe I'm not the prey, but the hunter."

"Huntress, I think you mean."

"Hunter, huntress, whatever. I just might be prowling, so don't worry about me." She straightens from the bar and starts past me back to the dance floor. "Just stay out of my way."

I watch the steady sway of her hips as she resumes her place on the dance floor, immediately joined by Mike Dunlov. The asshole.

"Hey, homey." I proffer a hundred-dollar bill to the bartender between two fingers. "This is yours if you can water down her drinks when she comes back for more."

His eyes widen and then crinkle with a smile while he pockets the cash.

"Sure thing." He pours vodka into a cocktail shaker. "I feel for her. I do all SportsCo's parties, and she and her fiancé were great together. It's only been a year since he passed. Gotta be hard."

"Yeah," I say without offering more.

I hate discussing her like this. I've found myself in three conversations about how she's handling her grief, and none of them with her. I know she's not ready for what I'm ready for. Hell, I'm not even sure I'm ready for what I think things could be with Avery. I don't have to be in her bed tonight, but I'd love to be in her head; to know what's behind that hollow laugh and that out-of-body look. Like she's here, dancing, drinking, flirting; going through all the motions, but she's somewhere else, alone and miserable. Not really here at all.

The deejay gears the tempo down again, and Sam Smith's cover of "Have Yourself A Merry Little Christmas" comes on. Avery freezes in the middle of the dance floor, but Mike Dunlov keeps rocking, talking incessantly, barely noticing that Avery stands rigid in front of him. He misses the look of absolute devastation that twists her expression and floods her eyes. She walks off, leaving him alone wearing his confusion all over himself. I follow her path past Mike and around the corner. A few feet ahead of me, she grabs a bottle of champagne from one of the servers and steps out of sight onto the balcony.

Cold wind slaps me in the face when I join her at the rail. Noticing gooseflesh prickling the skin of her arms and back, I slip my jacket off and drape it over her shoulders. She jumps, spilling champagne down the front of her dress.

"Shit." She holds the glass and the bottle away from her body, assessing the damage.

"Sorry." I pull a cocktail napkin from my pocket and pat the wet spot on the front of her dress. "Didn't mean to startle you."

With a half-hearted grin, she watches my hands moving over the scarce material of her bodice and skirt.

"If this is some elaborate scheme to get to second base," she says. "It might actually work tonight."

My hands pause just under her breasts, and I glance from the stain on her dress to the stain on her face. The stain of sadness with a shade of inebriation.

"As much as I'd like to take you up on your offer," I say, crooking one side of my mouth even though I don't feel like smiling, and it looks like she doesn't either. "I'll take a rain check."

She narrows her eyes for a second before shrugging, setting her glass on the balcony ledge and tipping the bottle to her lips, eyes never leaving mine.

"Some other guy's lucky night then," she drawls.

I grab her wrist before she can take another sip, and the rim of the bottle is poised at her lips.

"No."

It's one word, but it covers a lot. No, she doesn't need to drink anymore. No, it's not some other motherfucker's lucky night if I have anything to say about it. And no, I won't let her drown her sorrows in champagne and meaningless sex tonight.

"No? I'm a grown-ass woman, Deck," she snaps, a shadow flitting across her face. "Grown and fancy-free."

A lone tear streaks through her flawless makeup. "God, I hate this song."

I tune into the music drifting out to us from inside.

"Have Yourself A Merry Little Christmas"? I ask.

"It was his favorite Christmas song," she whispers and clunks the champagne bottle down on the balcony ledge. "It's awful."

She squeezes her eyes closed, but more tears slip over her cheeks. I want to put my arms around her again like I did at her apartment, but she's been so unpredictable tonight, I don't know how she'll respond. I hesitate, not sure what to say. I hate it when people say stupid shit to a grieving person. I don't want to be that guy, and I'm not known for my sensitivity.

"I know this is a hard time for you."

She stares at me, sadness and uncertainty suspended between

us like a rope bridge, before bringing the bottle to her lips and chugging without answering.

"Hey, hey." I urge the bottle down and away from her mouth. "That won't solve anything."

"Oh, you're so acquainted with grief, are you? That you know just what to do in these situations, huh? I'm so damn tired of being a situation. Of knowing everyone's wondering how I'm holding up, and wondering if I'm ready to date again. Wondering if I'm still . . ."

"Still what, Ave?"

She draws a deep breath and clutches the bottle to the smooth skin between her breasts displayed by the dipping neckline.

"You still on the top floor?" she demands. "Or has the network kicked you out already?"

"Nah." I draw the word out a little, buying a nanosecond to figure out where she's going with this. "I've got the penthouse for a few more days."

She nods, draws her brows together like she's processing what I've told her; like she's working out some problem. And then she says the words I would have given my first-year salary to hear the night we met, but now have no idea what to do about.

"Let's get out of here. Take me to your place."

Chapter 9

Avery

I know this is a mistake. I'm huddled in the corner of the elevator, my eyes fixed on the illuminated ascending numbers taking us inevitably to the top floor where Deck has been living the past few weeks. If I knew what was good for me, I would push the red emergency button; alert maintenance that there's an accident in progress right inside this elevator. But I can't. I woke up with this numbness spreading over my body like a plague. It's even frozen over my heart. I knew today would be painful; that it might hurt like a fresh wound, but nothing hurts and nothing feels good. Not the deceptively innocuous champagne bubbles zipping through my bloodstream. Not the many guys I danced with tonight or the secret touches they stole while we moved to the music. Nothing has made me feel all day.

Except him.

Call it lust. Animal attraction. Whatever it is, I felt it like a shot of adrenaline as soon as I saw Decker tonight. I study him from under surreptitious lashes, roving my eyes over silky hair the color of nutmeg brushed with honey. The slightest curl of it at his nape softens the hard line of his neck. His brandy-flavored eyes watch the climbing numbers, the bold nose and thick brows and wide, mobile mouth harmonizing his features into handsome. I study the impressive width of his shoulders and the bulge of his arms straining against the dress shirt. His jacket around my shoulders douses me in his scent and his warmth. I discretely snuggle deeper into its embrace, even though the arms hang limp and empty at my sides.

Yes, he makes me feel something. I want it to be as simple as lust; as the sad, horny girl who woke up with her dead fiancé on her mind and her hand between her legs, but it's not that simple. I've always known with Decker it wouldn't be.

"I don't think . . ." I struggle to wrangle my thoughts set on a wild goose chase by the alcohol I've consumed. "I'm not sure this is a good idea."

He looks at me sharply just as the doors open to his floor. We consider each other, neither making a move. The doors start closing and he catches them with one long arm.

"Come on." He tilts his head toward the landing beyond the elevator doors. "At least let me get some coffee in you. Sober you up and save you from bad decisions you'll regret tomorrow."

He thinks the bad decisions are back at the party with idiots like Mike Dunlov. No, the bad decisions are behind his closed doors, but I find myself half-stumbling after him to the penthouse. As soon as we're inside, I lean my palm onto the wall for balance and take off my stilettos. I lose another four inches, and now have to tip my head farther back to see his face.

"You're tall." I want to retract the obvious statement to a basketball player as soon as it trips past my liquor-loosened lips. Humor flits through his eyes briefly before concern swipes it away.

"Comes with the territory." He walks toward the small, neat kitchen. "Come on. Coffee."

I very carefully climb onto the leather stool at the counter, looping my bare feet on the slats. Decker makes even a simple task like making coffee look tantalizing. The play of muscles under his thin white shirt when he reaches for a mug. The efficiency of his big hands, quick and deft in the mundane preparations. There's a rugged grace to him; like rough metal that's been polished and chiseled until it gleams.

"You're beautiful," I blurt, causing him to stop what he's doing and stare at me.

I really *am* drunk. I'd never say that sober.

"Wow, you really *are* drunk." He echoes my thoughts, laughs and shakes his head, sliding the coffee across the marble counter top. "Drink this and I'm sure I'll be less beautiful soon."

I hope so because if he keeps looking like that, I can't be held responsible.

And isn't that what I want? For one night not to feel responsible? Not to feel guilty or condemned? Ashamed of my part in Will's irreversible decision? All night I've wanted to feel something, and in this moment, I feel everything. Like a wall dropped and every painful thought and emotion rushed in before I could get my guard back up.

"It's today," I speak into the quiet filled with only the hum of appliances.

"What's today?" Decker leans his elbows on the counter, gathering both huge fists under his chin and watching me closely, waiting for more.

I think he already knows. All night it felt like everyone knew I was desperate to forget the significance of this day.

"Um . . . a year ago today, Will died." I run a fingernail over the silky material stretching across my thighs.

"I'm sorry, Avery." Sincerity lays heavy in the dark eyes, unlit by his usual good humor.

"Did you know it was suicide?" The words cut my tongue like a razor. "That he took his own life? Right in our apartment."

"I didn't know. Did you . . ." His compassion reshapes to horror. "Did you find him, Avery?"

The horrible tableau plays out across my mind again like it has countless times before.

"Yeah." My whisper breaks. "I found him, but I was too late."

Despite the warmth of his jacket around me, I shiver like I'm back there; like the premonition that slid over me when I entered our apartment that night is revisiting my skin and reminiscing with my bones.

"Shit, Ave." Decker crosses around the counter to me, his taut stomach hitting my bent knees while I sit on the stool. "I'm so sorry."

"He was . . . he was . . ." My teeth rattle, shock shaking me like I'm standing in that bathroom again. "In the water. In our bathtub with so much blood."

Deck pulls me closer by the shoulders while tears course over my cheeks and dampen the fine cotton of his shirt. I can't catch my breath. Weeping quakes my body with the stupid tears I promised myself I wouldn't shed today. I was so determined to forget all of this tonight, and here I am, a sloppy mess all over Mack Decker. His wide, warm palms roll over my arms when his jacket falls from my shoulders and hits the thick pile carpet. He rests his hands at the curve of my neck and shoulder when my tears finally subside, his thumbs under my chin, lifting, forcing my eyes to meet his.

"Hey, you okay?" he asks softly.

I concentrate all my senses, all my focus on where his hands have been. My arms are warm from his touch. The sensitive skin of my neck tingles where his thumbs caress. The faint smell of alcohol and his expensive cologne flares my nostrils. My heart slams into my ribs like I've run and leapt and landed. Wordlessly, I scoot forward on the stool, widening my legs until he's between them, bracketed by my knees. The bold action forces the dress up to the juncture of my thighs, offering a glimpse of my black panties. His eyes drop between my legs and snap up to my face. He tries to step back, hands falling away and jaw ticking, but I latch onto one leanly muscled arm.

"Don't." I scoot forward more until I'm barely on the stool. "Please don't leave me like this, Deck."

"I'm not leaving you, Avery. I . . ." He gives a decisive shake of his head. "You're not in a good place tonight and I won't take advantage of that. I want to help you, not . . ."

His words trail away and his eyes are distracted, following a path along my collarbone, between my breasts, over my stomach and between my legs. I spread my thighs another inch, showing him what he's wanted for a long time and inviting him to take it tonight.

He licks his bottom lip, a fascinating swipe of his tongue that I lean forward and mimic with my own. His pleasured groan vibrates against my mouth, but he pulls back, drawing in a deep breath and shaking his head again.

"Ave, I—"

I grip him by the neck and lick the seam of his lips. His jaw drops on a gasp, and I push my tongue in, exploring the warm, silky interior of his mouth. My hands venture between us, finding him lengthened, hardened. When I squeeze, he growls into our kiss. His hands, which have remained in deliberate discipline at his sides, encompass my waist. They're so big his fingers almost meet at my back and his thumbs rest under my breasts. My nipples tauten in proximity to his touch.

"You're playing with fire here." His voice emerges rough as Brillo.

"I know exactly," I say, my voice husky while my hand pushes up and down over his dick. "what I'm playing with."

"Avery, we should—"

"Make me feel," I cut in, steadily pumping him through his pants. "You want to help, then make me feel."

Tears gather at the edges of my eyes, trickling unchecked over my face and into the corners of my mouth.

"Make me feel something other than pain, Deck." I meet his eyes, and they reflect my sorrow back to me. He groans when my hand persists.

"Promise me," he finally says, searching my face. "Promise me you won't regret this tomorrow."

A dissonant laugh flows out of me, misplaced in the grief and lust permeating the room around us.

"I can't promise you I won't regret this tomorrow." I stare back at him, not hiding my pain or my passion or my confusion or my need. "I can only promise that I want it like hell tonight."

Chapter 10

Decker

Avery's words, even more than her hand, grab me by the balls. The sight of her arrests my heart in my chest. I've wanted this woman for a long time, but knew it would probably never happen. Here she is offering herself to me on a very unexpected platter, and I'm not sure I can do anything about it. Because after all this time, I'll be damned if I'm settling for one night with her; some drunken memory she relegates to the back of a closet and never considers repeating.

"Deck, I just want to feel good." Her lips tremble when she presses them to mine again. "Make me feel. Make me come."

"Shit," I hiss at her brazen request. "Avery, I can't. Any night but tonight. I can't."

Surprise and hurt mingle in her dark eyes, calcifying into determination. She hops off the stool and stands, allowing no space between us so I feel the heavy heave of her breasts against my chest.

"Okay." She looks up at me, her mouth a stiff line set in delicate bones. "Maybe Mike can—"

"The hell Mike."

My hands clamp around her waist, stopping her from walking to the door. I swallow the last of my hesitation. She doesn't know if she'll regret this tomorrow. I'm almost certain I will, but I lose the fight with my will, with hers, and lift her back onto the stool. She wants to feel? She wants to come? Never looking away from her face, I drop to my knees and press her open. She doesn't resist. Her legs relax, stopping where I want them. I rub my stubbled chin and cheek along the sensitive skin inside her thighs, rewarded by the gasps above my head. The closer I get to my goal, the harder it is to breathe. The smell of her reaches my nose, unhinging my restraint. I tighten my hands around her thighs, forcing myself to go slow; to be gentle. I lift her legs over my shoulders, dragging her ass to the very edge of the stool to mouth her through the black panties. They're already damp, and her flavor seeps onto my tongue, so sweet I can't help but remember Sadie saying Avery could be my dessert.

"Oh, my God, Deck." Her words are needy and breathless.

I don't look up, too absorbed in the taste of her, even through silk. So potent. I nudge the panties aside with my nose, licking up her seam. She's wet and hot and tangy on my lips. I delve into her slickness, seeking out the crown jewel tucked inside, that cluster of nerves. I suck hard, and she bucks into my mouth. The steady interplay of tongue, lips and teeth at the intersection of her body and my mouth has her hips jerking and her hand clawing my hair. Her hips roll in tandem with me, and I glance up long enough to watch her inhibitions fall away. Her head drops back, the satin skin of her throat stretched and taut with pleasure.

"Deck, I'm gonna . . . oh God."

I slip two fingers inside, still sucking and licking while both her hands grip my head; while she commands me like a queen in her inner court. Her legs quake against me and her body tightens around my fingers convulsively as she comes. She rides it out over my mouth, taking anything I might not be giving her. Except I'm giving her everything, and she doesn't even know it.

When her body goes still, and the only sound in the room is our labored breathing, I slide away from her. That's as far as I'll allow myself to go. She wanted to feel. She wanted to come. I've done that for her, but I have to get her out of here.

"Don't, Deck." Her lipstick is smeared and her lips are swollen from our kiss. "Don't stop."

Her hips start rocking again like her pussy is remembering what I feel like; like she's seeking something. Seeking me. The panties still pushed aside, showing me how needy and creamy she is between her thighs. I'm shaking my head, a definite denial, but when she slides the shoulders of her dress away, her breasts are naked and perfect. Most nipples are small tight buds, but Avery's are lengthened and plump and plum-colored, resting at the tips of her breasts like heavy fruit on a vine. I want to drink. I'm already dizzy with the taste of her, but the sight of her unravels my convictions until they are shredded into ribbons at our feet. She stands, pushing at the skirt, sliding it over her hips and legs, a puddle of silk at her bare feet. She's only in the black panties, but even those she persuades down her body until she's naked for me.

She traces the tip of her finger over my eyebrows, down my nose, skims my lips, cups my jaw.

"You really are beautiful," she whispers, her eyes following the path her finger took. "Give me tonight, Deck."

I got nothing left. Any resistance melts under the awe in her eyes as she runs them over my face, as her look probes beneath my clothes. I want to show her. I want her to be as enamored with my body as I am with hers. I stand up, towering over her. I pull her bare back to my chest and walk us to the bedroom, all the way, cupping her breasts, pinching her nipples, caressing her stomach, pressing my hard-on into her ass, so that by the time we reach my bedroom, her breaths are ragged, her fingers trembling when she unbuttons my shirt. I stand perfectly still, watching her eyes glaze over with every portion of me she reveals. She fumbles with my belt, but I don't intervene, enjoying the clumsy brush of her fingers against my stomach. She opens my zipper, deliberately skimming a knuckle over me through my briefs, making my breath catch and cut in my chest. A little grin quirks one corner of her mouth when she sees my reaction. She pushes the shirt off my shoulders, leaning forward to suck my nipples.

"God, Ave." My fingers lace into the hair neatly gathered up, dislodging pins so it spills around her shoulders.

She shoves my pants down, following their path to my feet, settling onto her knees. Her velvety brown eyes peer up at me, hot and hungry, as she tugs my underwear over my legs, her hands tracing the muscles of my thighs and calves.

"Oh, my God." She stares at my dick, elongated and thick, bobbing at the entrance of her lips. "I'm not sure I can take it all."

"Won't know till you try." I line up with her mouth. "Open."

Obediently, her full lips part, and I push in, groaning every inch of the way.

"Mmmmmm." She clumps her eyebrows together, and for a moment I think it's too much; that it's discomfort tightening her expression. Then she lowers her jaw, taking me deeper into the tight channel of her throat.

"Mmmmmm," she spreads her hands over my ass, gripping as much of me as she can. She presses in closer, rubbing her breasts over my legs in sync with her mouth, sharpening her nipples against me, using me. It's turning me on even more.

"Shit, you give good head," I mumble, barely able to form coherent words. I bite my bottom lip until it throbs, a counter to the bliss happening below my waist.

She adds her hand to the equation, cupping my balls, pulling her mouth from the root all the way to the tip and insinuating her tongue into the tiny opening.

"Sweet mother of . . ." I grip her jaw, holding her at just the perfect angle, and fuck her mouth relentlessly, my hips a merciless cadence while tears streak over her face. I don't know if the tears are sadness, or if she's choking on my dick, but she won't let me go. Her fingers lock so tight on my ass, her nails dig into the muscles.

I will burst soon, and it will be inside of her. I carefully pull back and skim my palms over the fragile framework of her collarbone and shoulders, spreading my hands open, just whispering the palms over her nipples again and again. Her mouth drops open,

Kennedy Ryan

lashes fall to kiss her cheeks and she leans back onto her heels, pressing her arms behind her, the muscles in her legs strained, palms to the floor so she's offering herself to me. I keep working in tight circles over her breasts, and her hips jerk in time with my pace.

I lift her gently onto the bed behind us and spread her out, taking myself in my hand and pumping, making her wait. Making her watch. She moves her legs restlessly, looking for relief.

"Come on, Deck." She licks her lips, eyes fixed on my dick.

I straddle her hips with my knees, letting my cock rub between her legs in tantalizing swipes.

"Give it to me." She reaches for it, trying to line us up.

"You'll get it when I'm ready, Ave." My voice is hoarse and scratchy, and I want to be buried inside her, but draw it out for us both.

I take one nipple between my lips, varying the suction from gentle and barely there, to rough and aggressive. All the while pinching the other and rolling the nipple between my fingers. I transfer my mouth to the other breast and slide my hand, palm flat against her belly, between her legs.

She jerks when I peel back the lips and rub my fingertip over her clit in a swift rhythm. It plumps and tightens.

"Damn, you're wet," I groan, seduced by the sloppy sounds her pussy makes when I finger fuck her.

"I need it to be now, Deck," she pants, stretching her legs wide and tugging at my hips. Positioning me.

"Okay. Just one more taste." I want her juices on my tongue when I enter her for the first time.

"No," she growls, her eyes narrow and her face tight with passion. "Now."

I can't help but chuckle because she looks so fierce; so much like the girl who put me in my place at my locker. So much like the driven, ambitious, commanding woman I've come to admire from a distance over the last few years, even more up close the last few weeks.

"Now, you said?" With no more warning, I thrust inside, and

64

we share a gasp at the perfect fit. I know I'm big and she's tight as hell, but it feels perfect to me.

"You all right?" I crush the urge to slam into her, waiting for her to indicate it's okay to move. "Are you—"

"If you don't come on and fuck me, Mack Decker," she rasps, eyes half-mast and hands clenched around my ass.

My dick twitches inside of her at the coarse words, and she grins, locking her ankles behind my back. She better lock 'em. She has no idea how hard she's about to get fucked. I hitch an arm under her knee and grind in so deep my balls get wet.

Her eyes go wide, and her body moves up the bed with the first few thrusts. I pump into her at full force, rocking the headboard into the wall, making the mattress moan.

"Oh my God." One of her hands leaves my ass and grips the sheet at her side. "This is . . . oh my God."

I push her knees to her shoulders, folding her back, appreciating how pliable her body is under my hands. I glance down to watch myself enter and withdraw, watch the evidence of how much she wants me on my dick.

On my dick. Fuck.

"Condom." I pull out, and her face crumples.

"No, don't stop."

"Let me get this on." I reach into the bedside table, wrap it up in record speed, and get back in there, pulling her legs over my shoulders.

"Oh, yes." She links her fingers behind my neck and tosses her head on the pillow. She clenches around me, stiffens with wave after wave of her orgasm.

"I feel so much." She stretches her neck back, lifting slightly off the pillow. Tears slide over her cheeks. "Oh, my God. It feels amazing."

Her eyes meet mine in the dim light, and she shows me everything. The things she hasn't told me, the secrets that torture her. I may not have the words yet, but the feeling, the hurt shadows her pleasure and she tells me everything. The intimacy of it pushes me over, and I'm exploding, throwing my head back, gripping her hips, my body reduced to urges and instincts and thrusts and moans until I finish, sinking my teeth into the tender curve of her neck.

I roll onto my back, keeping her connected to me, staying inside of her, our bellies kissing. Her legs fall limply on either side of my hips. She pushes up onto her elbows to study me, tears spilling unapologetically down her face. Her mouth trembles, works around sounds for a few seconds before she speaks.

"You made me feel," she whispers. "Damn you."

And then she collapses onto my chest and weeps.

Chapter 11

Avery

"He left a note."

The confession slips seamlessly into the intimacy our bodies, maybe even our hearts, made in this bed. In the darkness of this room only brightened by the skyline twinkling beyond the window.

"What?" Deck adjusts me in the crook of his shoulder, kissing my temple and pushing my hair aside to nuzzle into my neck, too. "What'd you say, Ave?"

He sounds sleepy. We just finished round two, and I must say I've never been fucked like that in my life. It was . . . possession and dominance and tenderness and ferocity taking turns, all sides of him sharing me. I love the way he arranges me exactly how he wants, pushes my legs back just so. Tips my ass up to the desired angle. Spreads me to his specifications. And then fucks me like a train.

The man fucks like a train.

And I've been railroaded; possibly ruined for everyone else. If I had known there were men out there, fucking like that, I'd have a lot more notches on my bedpost in my quest to find them.

"Ave?" he asks again, reminding me of what I want to tell him, as much as I would love to stay distracted thinking of what we just did . . . twice. For the first time, I want to tell someone other than my therapist the secret I've been wearing like an albatross around my neck for the last year.

"He, um . . . Will, my fiancé. He left a note."

Deck shifts, carefully pulling his shoulder from under my head so he can lie on his side. So he can see my face while he waits for me to go on. I punish my lip trapped between my teeth.

"It was in the bathroom with my ring."

In the sliver of silence following my last words, I know he's mentally assembling the pieces of this puzzle before he asks his next question.

"You weren't wearing your ring?"

The question comes low and soft, a sympathetic query. Not a threat or an accusation or any of the things I've told myself I deserve.

"No, I had taken it off a few days before." I try to swallow, but can't past the scalding, swollen walls of my throat. "I . . . I . . . God, I . . ."

My breaths come in choppy heaves. I clutch the sheet to my naked breasts to keep my hands from shaking.

"Hey, hey." Decker cups my jaw in one big hand, brushing his thumb over the tears trickling down my cheek. "Baby, it's okay. Take your time."

It's been so long since a man called me "baby." Since I shared any intimacy with another person. Long before Will and I ended, our sex life dried up. The casual affection of intimate touches, naked skin, bared souls and endearments had long departed.

"I broke our engagement off a few days before he killed himself." The admission storms past my lips as if the words know this is their last chance; know that if they don't escape now I won't ever let them out.

Decker scoots down until his forehead lines up with mine, the height difference so great my feet stop at his knees under the cover.

"I'm so sorry." He dusts kisses over my wet cheeks, spearing his long fingers into my hair. "I can't even imagine. Tell me."

I stare through the dim light, searching his face for judgment, but it's not there; just a patient, waiting compassion. It gives me courage to go on.

"We had been over for a long time, I think." I squeeze my eyes tightly closed. "He suffered from depression. His medication made it so much better, but he didn't like to take it. Sometimes he wouldn't take it, and he wouldn't take care of himself. He'd lose friends. His work would go bad."

I lick at the bitter smile festering on my lips.

"We would go bad."

I shrug and shiver, pulling the sheet tighter around me. "I would say he wasn't trying hard enough. He would say I didn't understand. We'd . . . fight. We stopped . . ."

My voice dies in the dark. I dip my head to hide my face, ashamed to hear my part in this tragedy spoken aloud.

"You stopped what, Ave?" Deck probes gently, kissing my forehead and encouraging me to go on. "You can tell me."

"We stopped . . ." I glance up at him through a dampened veil of eyelashes. "We stopped making love. We were like roommates, miserable more often than not, but determined to keep trying. I loved him. I did, but I'm not sure for the last year or so that I was *in* love with him."

My harsh laugh puffs across our lips, just inches apart.

"Hell, he probably wasn't in love with me either there at the end," I say. "He went on a business trip and he cheated."

Deck's hard body goes still, and his thumb caresses under my chin, urging my eyes up to meet his.

"He was a fool," Deck says. "Not to speak ill of the dead, but anyone who isn't satisfied with you is a fool."

"No, I was a shrew." I wince, replaying some of our arguments. "We both wanted it to work so badly. We loved who we were in the beginning, but we weren't those people anymore. At least not to each other."

I always knew Will had . . . spells. Seasons when he would withdraw because life felt too hard, and nothing, not even our closeness, could pull him out. I didn't realize how bad it was until last year, and even then, I never imagined he'd harm himself. He stopped going to work. Stopped eating and showering regularly. Stopped making love to me. Stopped everything that made him happy. Stopped everything that made him . . . Will. He stopped everything that made us . . . us, and it broke my heart. Long before anonymous out-of-town hook up ho, my heart had been broken in minutes and hours and over days. We drifted out of love, into heartbreak, and settled into a terrible indifference. We were unrecognizable, and I didn't know if it would have happened eventually anyway, or if his depression, the wall it erected between us, forced us to it.

"So, what happened?" Decker prompts.

"When he told me he'd cheated, I. . ." I want to cover my ears against the memory of our raised voices; of our hurtful words. "I gave him his ring back. I told him it was over and went to a hotel."

Guilt assails me, fresh and wrenching. My heartbeat accelerates and my pulse pounds in my ears.

"That was the last time I saw him alive." I struggle to get the words out. "How could I do that, Deck? I knew he was depressed, was struggling, but I never thought he'd do something like that."

"Not your fault, Ave." He squeezes my chin between his fingers firmly. "Don't do that to yourself."

Doing that to myself has become a habit I'm not sure I can break. Blaming myself for what happened.

"When I broke it off, he thought I would reconsider, and asked that we not tell our friends and family yet so no one knew that just days before, I'd . . ."

Abandoned him. Left him on his own. Left him to die.

The details of that night overtake what I see, what I hear, hurling me back into that cold bathroom. All the sounds and images and horrors flood my memory. I'd gone to the apartment to tell him I was sure; that we should go ahead and tell everyone it was over. Not just because of him cheating, but because we weren't working anymore and hadn't for a long time. As soon as I let myself into the apartment, I'd heard the music drifting from the back to the entrance.

Have yourself a merry little Christmas

Let your heart be light
From now on your troubles will be out of sight

The closer I'd gotten to the bathroom, the louder the music became and the more I was sure something was wrong. The air trembled with it. Each lyric ached with the pain I'd seen in Will for years, ebbing, flowing, sometimes less, sometimes more—always there, but finally too much.

"He was in the tub," I whisper, my eyes unfocused on the room I'm in now, but seeing that other room; seeing Will in water turned scarlet with his blood. Seeing the deep lines sliced in his wrists, perpendicular to his pain; intersecting with the misery I'd seen in his eyes for months, but been helpless to soothe. I hadn't known his despair went that deep.

I still see that note, my name scrawled in Will's loopy penmanship. I still see the ring I had returned to him there on the counter.

"Avery, I tried," I say, my mouth trembling, an unsteady messenger for Will's last words. "That's all the note said. That he tried."

Was it an apology? For cheating? For giving up? Was it a condemnation of me, for underestimating his despair? For pushing too hard? For wanting too much? Always more from him, or for him? The questions make well-worn laps in my mind, round and round, dizzying me with the finality of Will's one-sided farewell.

The song. The tub. The blood. The ring. The note.

Second after painful second, I manage to drag myself out, like I've had to do so many times since that night. I focus on Decker, pleading for him to understand, or maybe to help me understand.

"Sometimes I'd say he wasn't trying because that's all I know how to do," I say. "I've spent my whole life *trying*. Achieving. Making things happen for myself, and on some level, I didn't understand that it wasn't that easy for him. That it wasn't about trying. It was deeper than that. For him it was harder than that. Maybe he was trying until he just couldn't try anymore. And I saw that too late, Deck, and now he's gone."

My shoulders shake with the emotion I've been hiding from for a year.

"When I saw the note, it had my name on it. No one else's." I shrug helplessly. "There was no message for anyone else, so I kept it to myself."

My laugh comes out hollow, barely a laugh at all.

"And if I'm honest, I didn't want anyone to know. To blame me like I blamed myself." I swipe trembling fingers over my wet cheeks. "God, I didn't want his mother to blame me like I blame myself. For her to think he did that because of me."

The words slip-slide on my tears, barely discernible, but Deck understands. He pulls me close, one hand stroking at the small of my back and one hand cupping my face as he kisses the wetness on my cheeks.

"Listen to me." His voice falls soft and firm over my hiccupping. "I don't know what you could have done differently in your relationship. When a relationship fails, we look backward with much more perspective than when we're in it. Believe me. I learned that after my divorce."

I sniff and nod against his chest for him to go on.

"And replaying our arguments and rehearsing our mistakes won't change how we handled things," he says. "But in a situation like that, you aren't responsible for someone making that decision. Our lives are just that."

He dips his head to catch and hold my eyes with his.

"Ours." He frowns, pressing his lips together over a sigh. "You remember that *Sports Illustrated* party a couple years ago?"

"Yeah."

We hadn't spoken, but I remember that lightning strike of seeing Deck again after so long. How my palms went sweaty and my heart went haywire and my stomach went all fluttery. I had seen him from time to time over the years from a distance, but that night, he'd been so close. Closer than he had been for a long time, and as much as I made sure nobody knew, it affected me. *He* affected me.

"I wanted your fiancé out of the way." His voice is gruff, prompting me to pull back just enough to see his face. "And I didn't care that I was there with Tara. I didn't care that you were with him. I'd wanted you for years, since the first time I saw you, and I resented him touching you. Resented his ring on your finger. I resented him having you when I never got my chance."

He pauses, a deep swallow bobbing his Adam's apple.

"I thought about that when I heard he had died," Decker says. "I felt guilty for even wishing him out of the way."

"But you didn't . . ." I pause to sort my thoughts and find the right words. "You had nothing to feel guilty about. Your desire for me didn't kill Will. He did that."

"Exactly, Avery." He brushes my hair back from my face. "Exactly."

His words sink in and I try to put myself in that place where I'm absolved of guilt. I can't quite do it yet. I know he's right theoretically, but that night I found Will wasn't theoretical. It *happened* to me, and I haven't gone a day without seeing him that way. Without asking if he was there because of me.

"I can't imagine how much pain Will was in to do something like that," Decker continues. "I assume it's something he wrestled with at other points in his life."

"All through college." I pause, before sharing another thing I haven't even told Sadie yet. "His mother actually told me his first attempt was in high school, and then again in college. I had no idea."

I shake my head, overwhelmed with how much I missed. "How did I live with him, share my life with him, wear his ring, plan our future and not know he'd tried to take his own life? Twice?"

"How would you have known if he didn't tell you?" Decker asks. "We hide in the open. We cover our scars so we can move on. Sometimes we hide because we're ashamed. Because we're afraid people won't accept us or love us or understand. No matter the reason, you didn't know. But even if you did, would you have stayed in a broken relationship for the rest of your life from fear that he would do something like this? These were demons he'd wrestled with before he even knew you, Avery. You can't take responsibility for his life, for his decision. You couldn't do it while he was alive, and you can't do it now that he's gone."

My therapist has said these things to me. I've replayed them to myself on days when I thought the guilt, the weight of his death would drive me mad. But there's a ring of truth when Decker says it that I haven't allowed myself to hear before. Maybe I thought I was letting myself off easy. In situations like this, you need someone to blame, and it feels wrong to blame Will. If I allow myself to place the responsibility with him for even a second, I become furious. I get livid with him for leaving me and his mother and his friends who care about him. Who love him and miss him and will live the rest of their lives asking the same questions I do.

Why?

How could you?

What didn't I do?

Could I have been enough to keep you here?

I want to throw things at the wall and I want to punch him in the face. More than anything, I want to rewind to an illuminating moment when I could have made a difference. I replay our years together over and over, watching from an objective distance, searching for that second when I could have looked in his eyes, seen how truly miserable he was with this life, and fixed it.

And maybe that's the problem. I've accomplished all my goals and created the destiny I envisioned for myself. A woman accomplishing what I have in sports and television is rare, much less a woman of color. I rose above expectations and limitations at every turn. I defied the odds. Every hurdle, I've jumped. Every problem, I've fixed. But I could never solve Will.

If you can't come through when it's life or death, when it counts, then what good are you?

I finally drift off to sleep in the rare comfort of someone else's arms and realize that is the question that's been haunting me. I may find no peace until I have an answer.

Chapter 12

Decker

I'm making French toast when she enters the kitchen the next morning.

She's not exactly shy, but she has trouble meeting my eyes. I hope it's just morning-after awkwardness, not regret. Last night was the best sex of my life. One of the best nights of my life period, even though there were tears and pain and it was hard.

It was *her*.

It was my chance to unwind the labyrinth that has been Avery all these years. To understand her and get a glimpse of what's beneath all that control. It's beautiful. So beautiful that now I'm addicted to her honesty and her vulnerability and her boldness and her brand of brokenness. If last night was my only hit, she's a high I might chase the rest of my life.

"Morning." I glance up from the toast sizzling in the pan.

"Morning." She toys with the belt of my silk robe she's wearing. The hem trails the floor behind her because there's more material than her much shorter body knows what to do with. It still looks really good on her, gaping in front, hinting at two high, perfectly round breasts and copper-toned skin stretched over a taut plane of feminine muscle in her stomach. Her hair, tousled around her shoulders, rests dark against the maroon-colored silk. She runs a self-conscious hand over the tangled strands, combing her fingers through and pushing them behind her ear.

"You look beautiful," I reassure her.

Her fingers freeze in the process of setting her hair to whatever rights she's attempting. She climbs up onto the high stool, leaning her elbows on the counter.

"Breakfast?" she asks unnecessarily.

I turn the toast with a laugh. "Looks that way."

She grimaces over my answer before surrendering a grateful smile when I pass her a cup of coffee.

"Sorry it's not your cold brew."

"It's fine." She takes a long sip. "Oh, God. Thank you."

She clears her throat, shifting a little uneasily on the stool.

"And thanks for the ibuprofen you left." She rims the lip of the mug with her finger, not looking up. "That was very thoughtful."

"You had a good bit to drink last night." I turn off the toast and start scrambling eggs in a second pan. "Thought you might be a little hungover."

A wicked smile starts in her eyes and then creeps its way to her lips.

"It's not my head that's sore."

I pause in the preparations, processing what she is saying. My laugh bounces off the kitchen walls and I walk over to her, notching my hips between her knees. My hands stroke her back through the silk. She's soft and warm and smells fresh.

"You showered?" I whisper kisses behind her ear.

"Yeah." Her answer is breathy. "Hope that's okay."

"I only hate that I missed it," I rasp at the fragrant, silky skin of her neck where my teeth marked her. "Sorry about this."

"My neck isn't sore either." She laughs, a liberated sound I want her to keep making.

"Oh." My hand wanders over her nipple and it beads under the silk. "Here?"

The slightest hitch of her breath is the only indication she's feeling this.

"No, not there."

"Hmmm." I pucker my eyebrows into a frown. "I'm running out of options."

I step deeper into the vee of her thighs until the robe splits and falls away, baring the toned length of her legs.

"Maybe it's here." I run one exploring finger from her calf, over her knee and inside her thigh, just shy of her pussy.

"You are getting so close," she says, eyes not leaving my face.

I slide a finger along either side of her clit, trapping it between the digits and then stroking it with my thumb.

"Shit," she mutters, her hips moving in the rhythm my fingers set. "That's it. Right there. Not a hangover. A fuckover."

I chuckle and stop my fingers, move my hand away.

"Oh, I'm sorry. If you're sore, maybe I shouldn't—"

"You should," she cuts in, returning my hand to her center. "Believe me you should."

And while our breakfast gets cold, I do.

———

Stretched out naked on my pillows, Avery licks sticky vestiges of syrup from her fingers, an empty plate in her lap and a sheet haphazardly covering her.

"That was good," she says, purring like a contented cat.

"Breakfast or . . ." I let my words trail off and I glance at the well-used bed where she writhed under me not too long ago.

"Both. Breakfast. Last night. This morning. All of it." She bites into the grin that graces her kiss-swollen lips until it fades with the careful look she angles up at me. "Thank you for everything. It was perfect."

We spent last night together, and half of today since breakfast became brunch the more we kissed and touched. And fucked.

Man, did we fuck.

And after just a day having her, it has been more intimate and more perfect than anything I experienced in years of marriage to Tara.

So the finality in Avery's voice wears on my nerves.

"You sound really grateful." I leave the bed, pulling on a pair of gray sweats from the floor and tying them at the waist. "What? You gonna send me a fruit basket or some shit?"

I meet her eyes head on, silently challenging her to tell me she regrets last night, this morning. That we won't pursue more. That it . . . *that we* . . . won't happen again.

"Deck" she starts softly, staring at her fingers toying with the sheets bunched at her waist. "We talked about this, about—"

"That was before," I butt in. "Before everything happened. Before we made love and we talked and we . . ."

I claw frustrated fingers through my hair. "Dammit, Ave, that was before and you know it."

"Nothing's changed." She scoots up to sit straighter against the headboard, gathering the sheet around her like forgotten armor. "I'm still as emotionally unavailable as I was at that party last night."

"Liar." The one word blasts into the chilling air separating us. "You were more available to me last night than any woman I've ever been with."

"I'm not talking about sexually, Deck."

"Neither the hell am I, *Avery*."

We glare at one another, our breath coming quicker with our mutual frustration. It's not totally unexpected, her withdrawal, but I thought I would have a little more time to convince her that we should try.

"I'm moving to California," I say abruptly. Her eyes widen before she catches the reaction and controls it.

"Oh, I thought . . ." She stops the nervous tugging of the sheets. "Oh."

"I told you my ex moved there. She keeps making it harder for me to see Kiera." I sigh wearily and scrub a hand over my face. "She's just pissed because she didn't get more out of the divorce."

"They say it's cheaper to keep her," Avery says with a cynical twist of her lips.

"Then 'they' don't have my lawyer or my pre-nup." We share a smile that comes a little easier to us both. "At the last minute, she pulled some crap so I have to go to LA to see my baby girl for Christmas, when she was supposed to come here for two weeks."

"I'm sorry, Deck."

"Yeah. So am I. It'll just be simpler for me to live out there." I hesitate for a moment before sitting on the edge of the bed, within touching distance if she decides to touch me. "I've been offered a front office position with that new expansion team the San Diego Waves. President of Basketball Operations, with the possibility of partial ownership eventually."

Ever the journalist, curiosity and questions stack up in Avery's wide eyes.

"And we *are* off the record, by the way," I remind her. "This isn't public yet."

"All right, all right. I get it." She pulls her legs up to her chest, resting her chin on sheet-covered knees. "Congratulations."

"Thanks. It works for me personally, so I can be closer to my daughter, and professionally because it's the kind of opportunity I've wanted, but didn't think I'd get for at least another five years."

"That's great, Deck." Her face has become the mask she showed me when we first started hosting her show together three weeks ago. "I'm happy for you."

"I don't want you to be happy for me, Avery. I want you to tell me that what we had the last twenty-four hours is enough to build on. That when I go away, we can try to build more."

"You saw me last night." Her mouth is the only thing wavering in her obstinate expression. "You know I'm a mess."

"We're all a mess." I scoot closer, palm her jaw and press my forehead to hers. "We'll figure it out."

She shakes her head against mine, not breaking the contact between our skin.

"There are some things I need to figure out on my own. Questions not just about Will, but about myself that I need to answer." She mirrors my touch, her hand cupping my jaw. "As much as I enjoyed last night, as much as I . . ."

She swallows, shutting her eyes.

"Deck, deep down you know I'm not ready."

I glance up to find her cheeks wet again, tears leaking from under her closed eyelids. I want to deny it. As much as I want to convince her that she is ready; that I'll make her ready, or be ready enough for both of us, I know it doesn't work that way. I still hear her sobs and feel her shaking in my arms, recounting the horror of finding Will in their apartment. I still hear her agony over his last words to her.

"Okay. I accept that you're not ready. I have to go to California, and I know you have to stay here in New York."

I dip my head to kiss her, coaxing her lips open for a languorous dueling of tongues that quickly ignites fire in me. In Avery, too, if her nails digging into my back are any indication.

I give her hair a gentle tug until she's looking deeply, directly into my eyes.

"The time may not be right, but we *feel* right, Ave. Tell me you see how right we feel together."

Her nod is the only answer she offers, sniffing at the fresh tears I know aren't all for Will. Aren't all for her. I know that some of them are for me. I bend to kiss her cheeks, darting my tongue out to gather the salt of her tears.

"Hey, look at me." I gently angle her face up so we have no choice but to see one another. "Promise me that when you have the answers you're looking for, that when you're ready, you'll find me."

She leans deeper into me, uncaring that the sheet drops, baring her stubble-burned breasts. She takes my mouth in a kiss that is part consolation, part declaration. She eases away, licking her lips like she can taste me there.

"That's a promise I plan to keep."

Chapter 13

Avery

"Are you sure about this, Avery?"

I ease into my cashmere coat and turn to face my mother.

"Yes, definitely." I pull my hair free of the collar. "Mrs. Hattfield only lives fifteen minutes away. I'll be back in time for dinner. Promise."

"It's not getting back I'm concerned about." My mother stares at me, her expression inlaid with concern.

"I know you lost Will, and he was your future. You loved him," Mom says. "But Will was her son. It may not feel like it now, but you'll find someone else. Marry. Have a family. You will move on. She only had one son. The pain of losing a child, you can't imagine it."

I finish tying the belt of my coat with slowed hands and a rapid heartbeat. Will wasn't my future. I wasn't in love with him, and it's a different man I already can't get out of my mind. The one who kissed my tears and rocked my world. I felt lighter after telling Deck the truth, and right now I want to tell someone else.

"Mom, there's something I haven't told you." A self-deprecating laugh escapes me. "Hadn't told anyone really until recently."

I get my nose for news from my mother. A journalism professor at Georgetown, it kind of broke her heart when I chose to attend Howard. She may have chosen the classroom, and I chose the field, but she still has the inquisitive mind of a journalist, and the questions gather in her eyes and between her brows as a frown.

"Okay." She leans against the stairway bannister in our foyer. "What is it?"

Considering how closely I've guarded this secret, you'd think I'd reveal it with some ceremony. Not on my way out the door with the car already running and warming up.

"Will and I, well . . ." I drop my gaze to the hardwood floor and tug at the fingertips of my leather gloves. "We weren't happy at the end."

I glance up after a few moments of quiet. It's not a stunned silence. It's a knowing one. My mother doesn't look surprised, merely curious, waiting for more.

"I suspected as much," she finally says. "I could tell as soon as I met him that Will was a sad man, but you made him happy. As happy as one person can make another, but ultimately our happiness doesn't hang on other people. We have to first be happy with ourselves, and I don't know that Will ever was."

Now *I'm* stunned. We haven't talked much about Will's suicide. Mom knows I found him in our apartment, but not much else.

"I was getting my things from the apartment because I'd broken off our engagement." The soft admission reverberates through the foyer. "I had agreed to wait to tell everyone. He wanted that, for us to be sure, but I was sure."

Rarely have I seen my mother truly off kilter, but I do now. Her mouth forms a little *O* of astonishment, before she covers it with her hand. She crosses the few feet from the stairs to reach me.

"Oh, baby." She takes my face between her hands. "I had no idea. You've been blaming yourself, haven't you?"

"Mama, he left a note." I lean into the soft comfort of her hand. "For me. It was just to me, and I never told anyone. I kept it. I didn't show the police or . . ."

A sob breaks free from my chest, and tears leak into her palm.

"What did I do?" I moan. "Did I . . . should I . . . I don't . . ."

"Shhhh." She pulls me close, the Chanel perfume she's worn for decades a reassurance that breaks whatever tendrils of control I have. My tears pour out, an unrelenting, inconvenient storm. "It's okay, baby. Let it out."

She rocks me in an ancient maternal rhythm that no one teaches; the same one she used when I fell and scraped my knee. When I experienced my first heartbreak. When I buried Will a year ago. After a few moments, she pulls away, hands on my arms so she can look into my face. I sniff and pass my coat sleeve self-consciously under my runny nose.

"No, honey. That's not how it works." She gives a sad shake of her head. "Will was obviously a troubled man, and I know it feels like cause and effect. Like you broke it off and he ended his life. We experience life, all of us, in the bad and the good times and the good people and the ones who hurt us. Everyone does. There are some people life is just harder for than others. Will was one of those, but you told me before how he struggled and didn't always take his medication."

"I don't want to make this about how he failed as a person. I don't want to blame him," I rush to say. "I'm not trying to ease my guilt."

"Well I am." My mother's eyebrows elevate. "Because you have nothing to feel guilty about. Will hurt in a way that we will probably never understand, and for that there is no one to blame. But there's a difference between blame and responsibility. We are each responsible for ourselves. And what Will did, he was responsible for."

That's a distinction I've tried to make to myself more than once, but I always seem to come back to my part in it, and anything I could have done differently. I nod, leaning forward to kiss her cheek before fastening the buttons left undone on my coat.

"I hear you, Mama." I walk to the door and give her one last look over my shoulder. "I'll be back."

"Hey, you aren't planning to tell Mrs. Hattfield that, are you?"

Was I? On some level, I feel like I need to get it off my chest; like I owe her an explanation.

"You told me," my mother says, gripping my hand. "I'm glad you did, because I think you needed that, but that situation is already complicated enough for her. Knowing you and Will broke up only makes it more complicated. May just make it harder, and right now she feels you are the only one in the world close to understanding her pain."

I think of our conversations over the last year. Not many, but each one, a release, a relief for us both.

"Don't take that away from her with information that makes no difference," Mama says. "That does no good. It might make you feel better, but it does nothing for her, and she's your first concern now. That note was to you and you alone. Private. I just want her to be able to move on and accept your comfort. It wasn't your fault. She'll know that, but knowing this would only raise more questions, and she already has enough of those."

I'm playing Mama's words in my head when I pull up to Mrs. Hattfield's. I park my father's Tahoe in the driveway, noting the dying rose bush in front of the house. The grass is longer than the last time I was here, even though it's winter. Her house, always neat and perfectly kept, appears slightly disheveled. I ring the doorbell, waiting. When there is no answer after a few moments, I walk over to the garage, peering in and finding the Cadillac Will used to tease his mother about.

"Are you a pimp, Ma?" he'd ask laughingly. *"Rolling around in your Cadillac."*

I mouth the words, smiling at the image of Will seated in the living room just beyond the doors of this house. One year we helped Mrs. Hattfield trim her tree. Will roasted marshmallows in the fireplace. His mother and I had hot chocolate, and Will had cider. My life with him rushes back to me in vivid detail; the colors, the scents, the touches, the laughs, the tears, the good and the bad. All of it inundates my mind and blurs my vision.

And I miss him.

Not all the hurt we caused each other at the end. I miss the boy I met at a public library, who crushed on me for years without letting me know. Who took me trick or treating with his twelve-year-old cousin for our first date. I laughed with my friends about it, but we all thought it was sweet.

"God, Will." I shake my head, blinking at the tears freezing before they fall. I turn to leave, my steps dragging toward Dad's SUV.

"Avery?"

I turn at the sound of my name, and Mrs. Hattfield stands at the front door, her chin wobbling and her face already streaked with tears. I run, avoiding little patches of ice, needing to get to her. As soon as I'm close, her arms stretch out and she pulls me into her. Her sobs vibrate into my chest.

"I miss him." Mrs. Hattfield weeps unashamedly, her head buried in the collar of my coat. "I miss him so much."

"I know," I whisper, my pain communing with hers. "So do I."

And it doesn't matter if I was wearing his ring. If we were lovers or friends at the end. If he cheated or how we injured each other. All that matters is that I loved him, and so did she. That besides the woman I'm holding, I was closer to him than anyone else on the planet. She and I knew his strengths and his weaknesses like no one else ever did, and can console one another uniquely.

We stand like that for I'm not sure how long. Long enough for the winter cold to bite through my gloves and whip beneath my coat. I pull back and look through the open front door. It's dark in there. No sign of life. No savory smells of food cooking or the pine scent of a live Christmas tree.

"Get your coat, Mrs. H," I command gently. "You're coming home with me."

I didn't get to tell my mom I was bringing someone home for Christmas dinner, but when I arrive, Mrs. Hattfield in tow, she doesn't look surprised and already has an extra plate at the table.

"How'd you know?" I ask her quietly while we set out side dishes.

"I know you."

She smiles, pride in her eyes that has nothing to do with

anything I've achieved or a goal I've crushed. She's proud of me for who I am, not for what I've done. Mrs. Hattfield and I share a tearful smile at dinner before we say grace. Still sorting through the tangle of guilt and shame and pain and fury, I hope one day soon I'll know me, too.

Chapter 14

Decker

"**I**'m stuffed."

My daughter flops onto the couch beside me in our hotel suite, curly golden hair fanning around her and onto my shoulder.

"Your eyes were bigger than your stomach," I reply, brushing the hair back from her face.

"Grams always says that." Kiera's eyes, the exact color and shape of mine, laugh at me from her mother's face.

"Sure does." I nod and sink deeper into the cushions.

"I wish we'd gone there for Christmas like we were supposed to," she says softly. "To Atlanta to see Grams."

My teeth clamp around the caustic response that springs to my lips. Tara, my ex, used some trumped up excuse about a cheer-leading camp Kiera is supposed to attend to make things hard for me. I suspect Kiera doesn't even care about the camp, but she loves her mother.

As she should.

I used to love her mother, too.

I guess.

Sometimes I'm not sure if it was love, lust. Habit? Whatever it was, in the end it wasn't enough.

"Next time." I shoot her a quick smile. "Maybe we'll go see Grams for Spring break."

She tips her head back and smiles wide, baring her braces, tracks of rubber banded metal glinting in the dimly lit hotel room. I glance at the silver domes covering the remains of our holiday dinner. Not exactly how I wanted to spend Christmas – in a hotel room on the West Coast when everyone who matters to me is on the East. Except my daughter, who matters most of all.

I wonder if it snowed in D.C. Avery's there at her parents' place. I promised myself I wouldn't think about her, but it's easier said than done when you wake up with a throbbing cock, an aching heart and one woman on your mind.

I pull my phone from the pocket of my jeans and open Instagram. She and the other SportsCo anchors are pretty active on social media. It's practically expected, and all of them post for holidays. No new posts from Avery for the last week, though.

"Who's that?" Kiera asks, leaning closer for a better look at the phone. "She's pretty."

I hesitate, never one to lie to my daughter, but unsure how to categorize Avery. If it were up to me, the answer would be easy. Obviously it's not up to me since she and I haven't spoken since that night in the hotel.

"Her name's Avery." I toss the phone on the hotel coffee table. "And we said no phones today, so don't go pulling yours out."

"You started it," she reminds me, eyes bright with curiosity and humor. "Drooling over your *girlfriend*."

"She's not my . . ." I stop myself because dammit if I don't *want* Avery to be my girlfriend. "She's a friend."

Kiera shrugs like it doesn't matter, but she's intuitive, sharp. I've had one-night stands and booty calls since Tara and I divorced, but none of it ever touched my daughter. She's never even seen me date or express interest in anyone, but she's picked up on my interest in Avery. She's growing up. I hate that our choices, mine and Tara's, in many ways made her grow up too fast and deal with things too soon. Like the fact that love isn't always enough. That sometimes it fades altogether, even for your parents, and it changes your world forever. I know how sad she was when Tara and I divorced; how helpless she felt. She tried to hide it, but it came out in counseling, and we've been open about our feelings with each other ever since.

"Hey. Look at me." I tip up her chin until our eyes meet. "Talk to me. If Avery and I *were* dating, how would you feel about that?"

She blinks a few times and lowers her lashes.

"It's cool." She presses her lips together tight before looking back up at me. "I mean, since you and Mom . . ."

There's a hundred hopes and a dozen questions peppered in the sentence she leaves hanging, and none of my answers would be what she wants to hear.

"You are the most important thing to your mom and me," I assure her. "We'd both do anything for you, but our life together, our marriage, you know that part's over."

"Yeah." The smile she offers seems hard to do. It's not easy. Not natural and mostly for my benefit. "It's cool."

I'm about to dig further when my phone vibrates on the table, drawing my attention and Kiera's. The photo, the contact's name, are clear for us both to see.

Avery.

I grind my teeth together and force my hand to remain still at my side.

Shit.

A week with no word and she calls when I've promised Kiera my complete focus. We agreed to silence our phones before dinner.

"You're not gonna answer?" Kiera asks. "Isn't that your girlfriend?"

"She's not—" I cut myself off when I see the laughter back in her eyes. "We said no phones."

The phone vibrates again, and I can only hope when I call Avery back after Kiera leaves, she'll answer.

"I'll make you a deal," Kiera says. "You get your call. I get my Candy Crush, and then we're back."

I calculate. Under normal circumstances I wouldn't release her from our bargain, but we've both been disciplined and maybe she deserves a little break.

"Deal."

I press the green button to answer my phone, but press it to my chest and give Kiera a wink and smile. "Love you, baby girl."

She rolls her eyes and glues her gaze to the phone already in her hands, but grins and mumbles, "Love you, too, Dad."

I step into the bedroom and close the door behind me.

"Avery, hey."

The silence on the other end swells, and I wonder if I caught the call in time or if she hung up.

"Av–"

"I'm here," she cuts in. "I just wasn't sure . . . I'm here."

"Oh. Okay. Uh . . . Merry Christmas."

"Merry Christmas to you, too."

The line goes quiet again. If she's unsure of where this conversation should go, I have suggestions. Number one being that we meet halfway between our coasts and screw all her doubts away. If she agrees to suggestion number one, the rest of the list becomes irrelevant. But I'm not suggesting shit. She wanted space, which I completely understand. As hard as it's been, I've afforded her that time. Ball's in her court. I remain silent, signaling that the next move is hers.

"I, um . . . I saw Will's mother today," she offers stiltedly.

There's a note of sadness, a familiar tremor in her voice. I can only imagine how hard that must have been. She has a lot to work out, but the fact that she's calling me after what had to be a difficult conversation encourages me.

"How was that?" I ask.

"It was . . ." In the pause that follows, I envision her shrugging and biting her bottom lip, dark hair spilling around her shoulders. I wish she was standing in front of me now so I could see if I'm right. "It was tough, but good for us both, I think."

Her chuckle comes across the line and warms me. "She was home alone and that just wasn't right. Will would have wanted . . ."

I'm waiting for her next words, but she lets out a frustrated sigh first.

"I'm sorry. The last thing you want to hear about is Will or his mom or—"

"I want to hear anything you want to tell me, Ave."

She pauses again, her sigh this time one of resignation.

"I didn't tell her about breaking up with Will or how things were between us at the end," she says. "My mother thought that might only make things awkward with the one person Mrs. H feels understands what she's going through."

"Your mother sounds like a wise woman," I tell her, keeping my voice even and free of anything that might shut her down. "So you told your mom? How do you feel?"

"Lighter. Between telling you and my mom, I feel lighter." Her laugh is a stunted breath of uncertainty. "Just seeing Mrs. H and crying and us both remembering Will the way we loved him, made me feel better. Does that make sense?"

"Of course, it does. You both probably needed some closure."

"You're right. Closure. I think I got some," she says and then goes quiet for a few seconds. "Oh, Deck, I'm just playing that back in my head and hearing myself. When I said I loved Will, I meant—"

"Whatever you meant is okay." I'm not that much of a selfish, jealous jerk to hold her feelings for Will against her. "Whatever you feel, or felt, is okay."

"Thank you," she whispers, so low I barely catch it. "I've been sorting it all out. I know we had something good once, Will and I, but you were right when you said I couldn't have stayed in that relationship. I think I'm finally starting to forgive myself."

She sniffs and clears her throat.

"And to forgive him. I've been so angry with Will, with myself. I'm getting there, but I'm still not . . . I'm not ready, Deck."

"For me, you mean?" I ask, my heart taking a nosedive.

"For us. I'm not ready for anything except tomorrow." Her voice wobbles a little. "And then the next day. And then the next. I need to take it one day at a time for a little longer. I still feel raw in so many places, but I'm getting there. I just think I'd be a hot mess if we . . ."

I gulp down the disappointment and clear my throat.

"Uh, yeah, I get that. Of course," I say, hoping I've disguised the deflation I'm feeling. "Well, I wish you the best and—"

"You *are* the best, Deck," she interrupts softly.

All the words I had queued up to assure her I understand why she needs to walk away from this, from us, wither.

"What does that mean, Avery?"

And why the hell did she call? Just to ruin Christmas? Mission fucking accomplished.

"I'm screwing this up," she says.

"Yeah, a little," I reply, a bit of bite in my words. "If you're just calling to let me down easy, you don't have to. We had a great night, like you said and—"

"I wanted to tell *you*," she interrupts. "Today felt like I had a breakthrough or something . . . shifted. Like I took steps forward when I've felt like I was standing still ever since I found Will. In some ways like I was still in that bathroom with him."

She stops to draw a deep, shaky breath.

"And you were . . . you were the only person I wanted to tell. To call."

Her disjointed explanation sucks all the air out of the frustration swelling inside me, diffusing the irritation and hurt – yes hurt – when I thought she called to stop what had barely started between us, but I desperately wanted to continue.

"I'm glad you had that," I reply simply. "And I'm glad you called, that you called *me*."

"I think I'll take more steps forward, and that I *will* be ready, but I want . . . I'm just asking for a little more time to clear this fog," she says. "I want to be healthy, whole, when we do this."

When, not if. Good sign.

"Are we ever really whole, Avery?" I ask. "If you figure that shit out, share your secret because most of us live with cracks. I had a career-ending injury, and it healed, but I'll never be the same. I'll never play ball again. Not the way I did before. That spot hurts like a summabitch when it rains. I don't know that I'd call that whole, but I'm walking. I'm not asking you to be whole. I just want to walk with you, baby."

"I think I can do that soon." Her words are so soft, but they fill my ears and land in the vicinity of my heart. "But I'm asking for the time to make sure. My last relationship turned out to be the worst kind of shit show, Deck."

"Ours won't be," I promise without hesitation.

I hear her breath catch, and I want to crawl through the phone, across time zones and kiss her senseless. Fuck her until she forgets everything but us. Fuck the fog away.

"I know it seems like this whole conversation has been about Will and my psychosis," she says, her voice dropping to a husky rasp. "But that's not the only reason I called. I can't stop thinking about you; about that night."

"Dirty thoughts?" I ask hopefully.

"Oh, God," she says with a breathy laugh. "You're ridiculous."

"And you're avoiding the question, Ms. Hughes. Have you or have you not been thinking dirty thoughts about me?"

"Filthy."

"Dammit, Avery," I mutter, running a hand over the back of my neck and glancing at the closed door separating me from Kiera in the other room. "If my daughter wasn't here—"

"Oh, I forgot, Deck. I'm so sorry for interrupting."

"Are you kidding? I'm glad you called. I've been thinking about you all day."

All week. Ever since.

"Dirty thoughts?" she teases.

"Hell, yeah dirty thoughts." I swipe a hand down my face, over my grin. "Filthy as charged."

"Keep it that way," she says, her voice softening even as it heats.

"Oh, what I'm feeling, it'll keep."

Chapter 15

Decker

"Who's next?" Seated on the couch of the San Diego hotel suite, I stretch my arms above my head.

"It's the last of the day." My assistant Marla looks up from my schedule on her iPad.

"Thank God for that." I crook a grin at her. "Is it too early to start drinking?"

"You drinking?" she scoffs. "What? One of your protein shakes?"

"That *would* be nice." My smile beseeches. "Could you?"

She rolls her eyes, but her smile is good-natured and longsuffering, two things anyone working with me needs to be.

"Let me get you set up for this last interview," she says. "And I'll run up the street to grab one."

"From that place I like, right?" I push my luck.

"Yes, from the place you like." She shakes her head and swipes across the iPad screen. "Gimme a sec and I'll brief you on this last one."

I've lost count of how many reporters I've talked to today for the San Diego Waves' media blitz. I, along with other front office executives, have made ourselves available to the press for questions about the new NBA expansion team, our draft prospects, and the upcoming first season. My canned responses have started losing their shine. The more tired I get, the more I feel like the jock still wet from the shower, no compunction giving half-naked interviews, and less like the guy in the suit scoping talent and making multimillion-dollar decisions. Thank God this is the last of the day.

"It's your old network," Marla says with a smile. "SportsCo."

I stare at her, my heart banging against my rib cage. I'm holding my breath like some lovesick chick waiting to hear Avery's name. She texted me congratulations when my position was announced, but didn't really engage much beyond that, even when I tried. Not that I've tried much in the last three months. She asked for space, and I've given it to her. Though I'm not sure how much longer I can hold out. We only worked in close proximity for three weeks, and we only had one night and a few conversations, but I miss everything about her. I lick my lips before I ask the next question.

"Oh yeah? And uh . . . who'd SportsCo send for the interview?"

"Huh? Oh. Lemme see." Marla trails her finger down the screen until she reaches the bottom. "Mike Dunlov. Ring a bell?"

"Sheesh." I suck my teeth. "Ring a bell? More like a gong. Can't stand that guy."

Disappointment settles on my shoulders, but I square them, refusing to droop. When she's ready she'll come. Avery's too strong-willed for me to force the issue. She knows how good we are together. She's told me more than once she needs time to heal, and I'm giving it to her. That's the thing with a full-court press. You have to know when to apply it, and when to let up, or it's useless.

When there's a faint knock at the suite door, Marla disappears from the sitting room to answer. I look up, grinning at Jerry, the cameraman who danced with Sadie at the Christmas party.

"How you doing?" I stand and wait for him to shift enough of his equipment to shake my hand.

"Good, Deck," Jerry replies with a smile. "Congratulations on all of this."

"Thanks, man. I . . ."

The words disintegrate from my lips and from my mind when Avery, *not* Mike Dunlov, walks into the sitting room with Marla. She looks beautiful as usual, but her hair is different. It's curly, the way I told her I like it. The way it was the day we met in the locker room. She gives me her professional smile, but there's a glint in her eyes that says she knows what I look like under this suit. We are intimately acquainted, and the closer she gets, the thicker the air becomes with our knowledge of each other. Unspoken, the memory of our moans, our rough fucking, our tenderness charges the room, and even though we're having a silent conversation, it becomes obvious that Marla and Jerry sense something.

"Uh . . ." Jerry's eyes move between Avery and me staring at each another. "Where should I set up the camera?"

His question jars Avery, setting her into motion. She assesses the room and directs Jerry. She doesn't look at me again until everything is set up and we're ready to begin. We maintain a friendly formality, just starched enough to be professional, but with the ease of former colleagues. I answer her questions patiently, forcing myself not to stare at her breasts, or the way her waist cinches, or the length of her legs. I don't stare at those things, but I'm *aware* of them. I remember what she looks like and I'm hard as a motherfucker by the end of the interview. To avoid the awkwardness of my hard-on, I stay seated when we're done and Jerry walks over to shake my hand.

"Good to see you again, Deck." He glances at Avery. "You ready?"

She better not go with him. I've been good, controlled myself and given her this interview, even gave her a scoop on things I told no one else. If she tries to leave this room, I'm tying her to the bed.

"Uh, actually . . ." She glances at me, a knowing grin spreading her full lips. "You go on ahead. We're done for the day. I'm gonna catch up with Deck for a little bit."

Or all night long.

Once the door closes behind Jerry, I just stare at her for a few moments, and she stares back at me. It's not awkward. It's anticipation, like we're not sure where to start first, but I just want to begin.

"I like your hair like that," I finally say.

"I know." She tugs at one springy dark curl. "I wore it like this for you."

"For me?" I lean back deeper into the couch, relaxing my legs so she can see the wood I worked so hard to hide from Jerry. Her dark eyes go hot, glancing from my lap to my lips. She takes a step in my direction.

"Stop." I release the word as a command. "There's something you should know before you come any closer."

She links her hands behind her back, pushing her breasts up a little in the silk top she paired with fitted slacks.

"What should I know?" She cocks one brow, waiting.

"Don't come if you're not ready." As much as I want her, as much as I've missed her, I mean every word. "If you're not ready to be with me, to *really* be with me, then don't come because I'm not used to settling, and I'm not starting with you."

She blinks rapidly over the surprise in her eyes, and takes one step in my direction.

"Anything else?" she asks. "Before I come to you?"

"Yeah, I'm not letting you go." I haul a hand through my hair, freshly cut for today's dancing bear media blitz. "Shit, Ave. I've been in relationships before. I've been *married* before, but I've never . . ."

I'm going to sound like a chick. I know it, but I can't stop the words.

"I've never felt like this about anyone else, and I'm not giving you up once I have you. You better get used to that."

Another step, and now she's close enough for me to see tears brightening her dark eyes.

"Is that all?" she asks, her voice rich with emotion.

I nod tersely, not sure she's taking me seriously, but wanting to touch her too much to press the issue. Taking the last few steps and stopping at my knees, she nods to my lap.

"May I?" she asks.

I scoot down another inch, making room for her body to settle over mine. She scoots up until her knees rest on either side of me, and leans forward, pressing her breasts into my chest and her elbows on my shoulders.

"Now let me tell you some things that *you* should know." She brushes a finger over my lips. "You should know that I have missed you every day we've been apart."

I try to ignore what her scent and her warmth and the force of who she is does to me; how holding her is the best thing I've felt since I left New York before Christmas.

"Have you really?" I ask, my tone casual, my heartbeat anything but.

She leans down until her lips hover over mine.

"I did," she breathes over me before going on. "You should also know that I've done a lot of thinking. My relationship with Will taught me a lot. I don't want another relationship . . ."

She doesn't want another relationship? Pain stabs me like a physical cut. Am I willing to be her fuck buddy? The itch she scratches whenever she needs it too badly to ignore?

No, the hell I am not. I make my eyes flinty for our stare off so she won't know she just hurt me more than any woman ever has.

"If this is just some elaborate bicoastal booty call," I say, starting to sit up and pushing her away from me, "Then you can just—"

"Shut up, Deck, and let me finish." She pushes my chest so I fall back onto the sofa. "As I was saying before I was so rudely interrupted."

She pauses to lift one brow. "I don't want another relationship *like I had with Will.*"

Her eyes soften, the brown darkening with emotion.

"I want a relationship where I don't hide and neither do you," she says. "Where we trust each other even with the hard things; the things that break our hearts and cause us pain."

"Avery—"

"Where I never have to worry about you cheating on me and you never have to worry about me cheating on you," she continues.

"Where even if we're three thousand miles apart, we're as close as two people can be."

Hope climbs up my chest. I was afraid to let myself hope, but she's here and she's ready, and I can't keep my hands off her even for another second. I grab handfuls of her ass and press her down onto me. We both pant at the first grind of her body into mine.

"That all sounds doable," I rasp.

"'Doable?'" she asks breathlessly. "I'm risking a lot here. I'm gonna need something more definitive."

"Really?" My hand moves between us until I can get down her pants, past the barrier of her underwear. She's wet and slick under my stroking fingers. Her hips rock into me, and her head drops back. With my free hand, I loosen the buttons on her blouse. It falls back to reveal a flesh-colored bra of such thin lace I clearly see her nipples.

"I love how big your nipples are." I suck them through the lace, my mouth an eager suction. She moans and slides urgently over me, seeking friction.

"Dammit, Avery, don't make me fuck you like this," I mutter, eyes clenched closed. "I wanted flowers and candles and all kinds of romantic shit when we did this again."

"Fuck flowers." She deals with my belt and slides my pants down, barely waiting for me to lift my hips to help her. "There will be plenty of time for that. Right now, I need you."

She pauses, swallows, her eyes filled with passion, affection and . . . more. I'm afraid to name it, but there is more there.

"I need you," she says again.

"I'm right here, baby." I slide her pants and panties off.

She takes me in hand and pushes down, her walls clinging to me.

"Oh, God." Her head drops back. She rises and falls over me. "Yes."

I slide the cups of her bra over her breasts urging her forward for my bites and licks.

"Shit," I mumble against the silky skin. "Avery, it's been a long time. Slow down or this'll be over before it starts."

She pauses, looking down with a smug grin. "Exactly how long are we talking?"

"If you're asking if I've been with anyone since Christmas, since you." I thrust up, hard and sure. "The answer is no."

I grip her hip, commandeering the pace from beneath her.

"And if you've been letting anybody else in this pussy," I say with grave seriousness. "It's better you don't tell me because that motherfucker might end up dead."

Her husky laugh breathes over my lips.

"No other motherfucker's been in here."

"Shit." I grimace my frustration. "Why can't I remember a condom with you?"

"It's okay." She leans her forehead into mine. "I'm clean and safe."

I get to fuck Avery raw? I might shed a tear before this is all over.

"Yeah." I nod quickly. "Me, too."

A salacious smile curls her lips. "Then let's go."

She resumes the ride, her face twisting with the effort, with the grind. I flip her onto her back. Eyes locked, we fuck so hard the couch is scooting with the vigor of it. Just inches scraping across the floor, but the sound of it turns me on even more.

She anchors her feet at the small of my back.

"Shit, shit, shit," she chants, eyes rolling back. "Harder, Deck."

"Fuck, baby," I mutter. If I go any harder, I'll break her, but I take her word for it and as soon as I thrust harder, go deeper, her scream pierces the luxurious quiet of the suite. And I'm not far behind, falling over a cliff into the hottest, wildest, longest orgasm of my life.

We lie there on the couch, hot and sweating and panting, laughing between kisses until our stomachs growl. Who would have thought that first night in the locker room all those years ago, that we'd end up like this? We spend the rest of the night feeding each other from room service trays, bathing together, making love, making plans, making promises. Sharing hurts, shedding tears, and loving. Yeah, the words aren't said, but it's there, and we have all the time in the world. For me, there's no doubt it's there. We've both had suffering mixed in with love. We've loved and lost and were never satisfied. But I'm satisfied with her, and I see in her eyes that she's satisfied with me. We both have pasts and we've both had pain, but what we've never had was each other.

But now we do. Thank God, now we do.

Epilogue

Avery

It's Christmas Day, and in D.C., my parents are shoveling snow from the sidewalk. That was me a year ago today. This year, in beautiful stark contrast, I'm watching azure blue waves lick at golden sand. I lean over the balcony to wave at the little girl and older woman down on the shore collecting seashells.

"I'm a lucky bastard," Decker says from behind me, wrapping his arms around my waist and tucking me closer into him. "All my girls under one roof for Christmas."

I turn to face him, reaching up to fiddle with the collar of his shirt.

"Your mother is amazing." I trace the bold planes of his face with one finger. "Now I know where you get those eyes."

"Hmmmm." He bends to kiss the curve of my neck.

"And Kiera is so beautiful." I bend my neck back, giving him better access. "I'm so glad she's spending Christmas with us."

"I'm glad *we're* spending Christmas with us." His big hands slide down my back to squeeze my butt. "This ass. Don't ask how often I think about your ass when we're apart. I might creep you out."

"If I wasn't creeped out by you flashing your junk at me the night we met," I say, laughing against his chest, drawing in the familiar scent of him. "I think you're probably safe."

"Then we won't talk about these either," he says huskily, pushing aside the lapels of my dress to suckle my breast through my bra.

"Deck." I gasp and clutch his head tighter to me, starting to rock my hips into him in rhythm with his mouth. A seagull's squawk reminds me that, though Deck's beachfront property is private, we're still out in the open. "We have to stop, baby."

"I need you." He growls into the cleave of my breasts before righting the dress. "Stay an extra week."

He knows I can't. The interview I've scored with one of the world's best soccer players is a huge coup. Unfortunately, the interview is in Brazil at the beginning of the year.

"We get seven whole days together," I whisper into the tanned column of his neck. "And we have so much time to make up for."

His sober expression doesn't lighten, and I shake him a little, offering a smile to cajole him into a better mood.

"Deck, come on. You came to D.C. to meet my parents at Thanksgiving. I'm meeting Kiera and your mom for Christmas." I cup his jaw, forcing him to look at me. "We're making this work."

"But when do I get you next?" He laces our fingers together. "The season is about to kick into full gear. It's our first year, so I know we won't make the playoffs, but we're doing better than expected, and I can't let off the gas. My travel schedule—"

"Is part of your job," I cut in. "Just like mine is. We'll see each other every chance we get. That's what we've been doing, right?"

I once dropped everything and raced to LaGuardia where Deck had a layover. We only had an hour, but we made the most of it. I can now say I've been fucked in a men's bathroom. Hard.

No regrets.

"I just want this so bad, Ave." He rubs a thumb over my lip, leaving a trail of tingles. "I want this to work."

"It is working." I tip up on my bare toes to string kisses along his jawline. "We're working, Deck."

"I know, but it could be easier. SportsCo has an LA office," he reminds me, glancing up through those thick lashes. "Couldn't you . . ."

He trails off because we've had this discussion more than once.

"They do have an LA office, but right now they want *Twofer* based in New York." I pause significantly. "I know because I asked."

He pulls back, surprise and pleasure mingling in his eyes. "You asked?"

"I want this to work, too, Deck." I blink at the emotion that overtakes me when I think about how patient he's been the last year. How he helped me so much as I got past Will's death. "I want us to work so much. I love..."

I catch myself. What the actual fuck? We haven't said those words yet. I know them. I believe them. With every fiber of my being, I believe them. I can't imagine spending my life with anyone else, even if right now thousands of miles separate us most of the time. But that's a big step. Those words are a huge step, and the last man I gave them to broke my heart in the worst ways with the worst goodbye I could ever imagine.

Deck doesn't look thrown off by my slip, but just tucks my hair behind my ear and smiles down at me. I know he loves me. His eyes glow with it. I think the only reason he hasn't said it yet is because he wants me to be sure. He knows how fragile I was after Will, and he's handling me like glass.

Not in the bedroom. In bed, he fucks like an animal, and gets no complaints from me.

In every other way, he's been extraordinarily careful with me; extraordinarily patient. And, yes. I love him for it.

I brace my hands on either side of his face, and lock my eyes with his, losing myself in the intoxicating bourbon of his gaze.

"I love you, MacKenzie Decker," I say, my voice, my eyes, my heart steady and unwavering.

He swallows deeply. His hands tighten at my waist, feeling like they'll crush me, but I don't even whimper. I want to feel him any way I can.

"Avery," he finally says. "Baby, I love you so much sometimes I think I'm gonna explode with it."

He dips his head into the curve of my neck, feathering kisses there and into the collar of my dress.

"And I know I'm demanding," he goes on. "Always asking for more of your time, for you to come here more, to meet me on the road. It's not fair—"

"You come to me, too. You travel constantly. I'm always working. We have busy lives, but call me, and there's no place I won't come. This relationship is important to me." I kiss his cheek, scrunch my fingers in the silky gold-dappled hair. "You know that."

"I do know," he says, his eyes earnest, sober, loving. "And I don' t take it for granted. I want to make you happy, Ave."

I learned from Will that happiness starts with yourself; that your happiness can't truly hinge on one other person in this world. In the end, other people can't complete us, but can love us in our brokenness if we let them. There is a happiness you find with another when you're first happy with yourself. The joy of shared struggles and ups and downs and trials and *I'm there for you*, and *you're there for me*. It makes the contentment you find first with yourself even brighter, even deeper. And as we hold each other, the cool beach breeze blowing gently over us, I'm reminded of Deck's patience as I figured that out; as I dragged myself out of the mire of guilt and shame and pain.

I have no doubt that's the love Deck and I share.

"I am happy, Deck." I snuggle deeper into my big man, his arms wrapped around me and sheltering me from the whipping breeze. "I'm already happy."

FAST BREAK

"Throw away the idea of 'getting back' to your life as it was, and embrace the idea of 'stepping into' life as it is and all that it can be."

– **Amy Purdy,**
Paralympic snowboard medalist,
New York Times **Bestselling Author &**
All-Around Bada$$

Chapter 1

Ean

"**Y**ou can do it until you think you can't."

I consider the young, eager faces assembled on the bleachers of the outdoor basketball court. They're sitting in the mild San Diego summer sun, guzzling Gatorade and water, sweating and winded from the pick-up game they just finished. August West, the franchise player for the team I coach, sponsors this basketball camp. It's one of my favorite things to do in the off-season.

"The point of position-less basketball is teaching you flexibility, versatility," I continue. "How did you feel when you had to play a position you weren't used to?"

There's that "play it cool" silence when guys aren't sure they want to participate; don't want to seem too interested. I fold my arms and watch them steadily; let them sit in it for a few moments until one of the players I saw take the lead on court takes the lead here, too.

"Frustrated at first," Lorenzo finally says. "I never played forward. I'm a guard."

"That's to be expected." I cup the basketball against my hip and tap a clipboard on my leg. "You're asking your mind and body to function in ways and in situations they haven't before. How'd you feel by the end of the game?"

"I dunno." Lorenzo shrugs and grins. "I'm always gonna be a guard, but if I have to play the three, I can."

"Right." I bounce the ball with my left hand and nod. "You guys remember when Magic Johnson demonstrated maybe the best example ever of the position-less mindset?"

There's no recognition on any of the fifty or so teenage boys' faces.

"Come on now," I scoff. "You guys aren't *that* young, are you?"

They snicker. Some lean forward, elbows on their knees. Others lean back, elbows against the bleacher behind them. There's barely peach fuzz on their faces, so I guess they really are that young. Or I'm that old. At forty, I'm one of the NBA's youngest head coaches, but looking at these bright eyes and their spit-shine hope, I could easily feel like an old man.

"So the year was nineteen-eighty," I begin.

"Damn, I wasn't even born yet," Coop, one of the group's centers, says.

"I hear ya," I laugh. "But knowing the history of this game is as important as what you do on court."

My coach told me that when I was the same age as these guys. I had to live a little before I appreciated that and most of the things he said, but I'll tell them now anyway.

"It was the finals. Lakers were leading the Sixers, up three games to two. They were on the road, and they could close the series. Kareem Abdul-Jabbar was stuck in LA with a sprained ankle, and the championship was on the line. Magic Johnson, a rookie point guard, not only played center in Kareem's place that night, but rotated to play all five positions over the course of the game."

They seem suitably impressed, which spurs me to finish the story. "He scored twenty-five points in the second half. Thirty-seven overall. And as a *rookie*, he led his team to his first championship. Position-less basketball at its best."

A quick survey of the group makes me think maybe the

example isn't falling on deaf ears. They look invested and on the edge of their bleachers.

"Part of why I asked you to do that was because it's a great exercise in taking what might be considered a disadvantage and converting it into an opportunity to grow."

August walks up beside me and clasps my shoulder.

"Give it up for my coach, guys," he says, pausing for their applause. "Coach Jagger's talk is a perfect segue into our next guest. She has inspired millions with her tenacity and doing exactly what Coach was just talking about. Taking what some might see as a disadvantage and using it to grow. Quinn Barrow's gonna chop it up with us after we take a quick break."

The kids disperse, heading back into the air-conditioned building where I presume the next segment will take place.

"So Quinn Barrow, huh?" I ask, keeping my tone nonchalant. "I didn't know you were having her today."

"What?" August asks absently, squinting at the group of boys filing into the building. "Sorry. Making sure nobody's sneaking off. What'd you say?"

"Quinn Barrow," I repeat patiently. "She's speaking?"

"Yeah, Banner hooked us up."

Banner Morales-Foster is a partner in Elevation, the sports agency that manages August and several of my guys from the San Diego Waves squad.

"She's something else." I fall into step beside August as we walk through the parking lot.

"Uh, Jag." August glances over his shoulder in the direction we just left. "Wasn't that your Rover we just passed? I thought you had to leave for another appointment."

I pull my phone out and, as discreetly as possible, text my assistant asking her to cancel my lunch meeting with Body Armor. I've wanted to meet Quinn for a year. I'm not missing my chance.

"Cancellation." I wave my phone at him. "Just got a text from my assistant, so I can hang for a little bit."

"Cool. You got time to hear Quinn? She's a pretty fantastic speaker."

"You know I'm always looking for anyone to motivate the team."

"Yeah, maybe you can ask her about coming to speak this season," August says, opening the door to the building the kids entered. "She donated her time for the basketball camp, but the Waves would have to pay. And she ain't cheap."

Cheap isn't a word anyone would apply to the woman standing at the front of the room. Her green dress, well-cut and fitted, hangs from skinny shoulder straps and dusts the tight curves and delicious swells of her body, stopping just below her knees. She hops up onto a table, facing the roomful of young men. She even smells expensive. Her scent cuts over the smell of teenage boy. Something clean and fresh and sharp and citrusy.

"Our next guest is a *New York Times* bestseller," August says. "She owns a hugely popular gym in LA called Titanium, recently released a brand-new fitness app, is an international speaker, and has an Emmy-nominated Netflix special. Please give a warm welcome to Quinn Barrow."

I lean against the wall in the back of the room, clapping along with the guys and waiting for Quinn to begin. I've seen her around the stadium at games a few times. Seen her on television. I bought and read her book. Watched her TED talk. I know her fitness app is called *Girl, You Better*, and I'm not exactly the target demographic, but I downloaded it anyway.

She fascinates me.

They call me The Machine because of my obsession with stats and data. I have a reputation around the league for being taciturn. Reserved. Hell, maybe even reclusive.

I'm a gym rat. If I'm not at the gym, I'm at home. This job, this game consumes your entire life. I have a lot to prove. Coming off our first playoffs appearance, I'm chasing a championship ring. There isn't room or time for much else, and honestly I haven't *wanted* much else. But finally seeing Quinn Barrow in person, I want to get to know her.

"Good afternoon," she says, still seated on the table. "I'm honored any time I get to speak to young athletes."

There's an electric charge in her voice. Like she's plugged into a wall socket and can barely contain the power surging through her. Her voice pulses with it. As she looks over the small crowd, that energy illuminates her features. Facing this group of eager kids, it looks like someone just turned her light on, and she glows.

"I sat where you are once," she continues. "I knew exactly what my life would be. I had it all planned out. I was a world-class runner, and my future depended on how fast and how far my legs could take me. I had set records and was at the Olympic trials when everything changed."

She runs a hand brusquely through her hair. "I was running a great race, leading the pack, and on course to set a record at the trials," she says. "I heard a pop, and next thing I knew, I was on the ground. Runners fall all the time. I mean, it sucks at the Olympic trials, but it's not unusual. But this wasn't your average fall. Turns out I had dislocated my knee and ruptured the popliteal artery behind it."

"Did it hurt?" Coop asks.

"God, yes." Quinn closes her eyes and blows out a quick breath. "Like hell. I actually blacked out for a minute. They took me to the hospital, but didn't figure out the rupture right away. My calf and all behind my knee started turning purple. By the time they realized blood wasn't circulating to my lower leg and toes, it was too late."

She bends, working her fingers under the hem of her dress for a second, tugging and pulling her left leg away from the knee. She holds it up for the group to see, a prosthetic leg tipped with a red-bottomed shoe to match the one she wears on her right.

"Shiiiiiit," Lorenzo says, stretching the profanity to its limits.

"My thoughts exactly." Her grin, wry and small, comes and goes. "They performed six surgeries trying to save my leg, and one finally to take it."

Her tone remains light, her demeanor matter-of-fact, and everything about her proclaims unshakeable confidence, but she's holding her leg in one hand. And as the room is so quiet, waiting for her to flip to the next page in this tragedy, I can't ignore that empty space beneath her skirt where her hopes and dreams used to be.

"When I woke up after the surgery," she says, looking from the prosthetic to the group, "I thought my life was over, but sometimes life has a way of flipping our dreams upside down to get them right-side up. I'm not gonna sugar coat it, because you deserve the truth. I tried to end my life."

She holds up two fingers, and a crooked railroad track of scars cuts across the inside of her wrist.

"Not once, but twice." A philosophical shrug lifts the slim shoulders beneath the silky ribbons securing her dress. "I was nothing if not determined, and I was in the darkest place I've ever been in my life. The career I'd been pursuing literally since I was a little girl was gone in an instant. I didn't know how to be anyone other than that person. That led me down such a dark path."

"What saved you?"

I'm surprised the question actually left my mouth. I don't regret it, though, because she looks at me for the first time, right in my eyes, and I'm glad I stayed.

"I saved myself," she replies softly, her stare affixed to mine. "But someone else helped me believe my life was *worth* saving. Banner Morales-Foster, my agent and best friend, didn't know me from Jane Doe at the time, but she visited me in the hospital after my second suicide attempt. She told me I would run again, and that there was something special in me that she wouldn't give up on. She said she could see me speaking before thousands of people. She cast a vision that at the time, I couldn't even imagine for myself."

Quinn touches her left thigh, her hand moving over the muscle beneath the silky material of her dress. "I couldn't even walk, much less run, but everything she said, we've made come true. Most would call me disabled, but losing this leg *enabled* me, forced me to stretch so far beyond what I ever thought I'd be able to do. Probably beyond what I ever would have done."

Over the next twenty minutes, Quinn recounts her unlikely rise from that hospital bed to bestseller lists, endorsements and being a household name. At the end she brings out a case with various types of prosthetics for the guys to see, ranging from those that look like flesh to those that shine with sleek steel.

"So do you have a favorite?" I ask from beside her while she arranges them on the table.

"For events like this, I like the one I'm wearing," she says, chuckling. "I can show off my extensive shoe collection, but running, I'd go with something like this."

She reaches for the C-shaped blades I've often seen amputees run in.

"They're lighter." She hands one to me to feel and then another heavier leg for comparison. "And the blades mimic how our tendons work. The inventor was inspired by the way cheetahs and kangaroos run as he was designing them."

"So you run a lot?" I'm running out of things to say, but I want to keep her attention as long as possible. I'm distracted by the sexy slope of her shoulders under the fragile ribbon straps, and the vulnerable sweep of her neck when she seems so strong everywhere else.

"Yeah. Most mornings I do." She opens her mouth to say something else, but Coop asks her a question about one of the prosthetics. She walks around to the other side of the table where he's standing and launches into an explanation.

Dammit.

I'm not sure how much longer she plans to stay. I don't usually . . . linger in places. When I'm done, I'm out. August knows this, and his speculation reaches me from across the room. I'm not surprised when he sidles up beside me.

"You still here, Coach?" he asks. "Thanks for hanging around so long."

"It's nothing." I shrug, my shoulders stiff, trying to look natural and casual. "The kids are great."

"So's Quinn, right?" August elbows me in the ribs. "You should ask her out."

I freeze and issue him the wintry look I usually reserve for chewing him out when he's slow on defense.

"What'd you say to me?" I ask, my voice low and cool.

"Um." August bites his lip, but his smile still breaks through. "I just noticed you keep watching her and kind of . . . following her around the room, so I thought maybe you should ask her out."

"I'm not following her around the room."

"Uh, yeah. You kinda are." August's smile fades. "Seriously, Coach, you never go out. I have no idea who your friends are. Your whole life is on that court. I'm not one to give advice—"

"And yet I'm getting this misplaced wisdom vibe."

"But," he says pointedly, ignoring my comment, "I've learned a thing or two about having a life outside the gym. I highly recommend it."

August is nearly fifteen years younger than I am, but he already has a wife, two kids and a beautiful home in San Diego. I haven't slowed down long enough for any of those things. Nothing has made me *want* to slow down.

Quinn's husky laugh drifts over, and she seems as much at ease in a roomful of teenage boys as she does on the set of *The Tonight Show*. I admire everything I know from her public life. This brief glimpse of her in person has impressed me even more. She turns my head. She speeds my pulse.

She makes me want to slow down.

"I need to go get these guys set up for their afternoon drills," August says, walking backward and shrugging. "I'm just saying, what do you have to lose?"

Little things like dignity and self-respect.

"Bye, guys," Quinn says, waving as the group trails out after August and to their next activity. She starts packing the prosthetics into cases.

"You're alone?" I ask. "I expected you to have an entourage."

She snorts, steadily sorting the legs into sections of the cases. "No entourage. Especially for something like this—a quick drive down from LA and a group of kids. I like to be on my own if possible."

By the time she's done there are four cases, which look pretty heavy.

"You brought these in by yourself?" I ask.

"Now that I think of it, August helped me load in, but I can manage."

"You don't have to," I say, grabbing three of the cases and leaving one for her to carry. "My mama would skin me alive if she knew I'd allowed a lady to walk to the car with all that stuff by herself."

"This lady would have been just fine. I have a tendency to figure things out for myself, but thanks for the help."

We exit and a comfortable silence falls between us. We're almost at the parking lot and I haven't done more than assert my good home training. I wasn't this pathetic asking a girl to the seventh-grade dance. My mind is like an open field right now, and I can't pluck one thing to talk about.

"I'm Ean, by the way."

"I know who you are." She laughs. "You're head coach now, right? Not assisting anymore for the Waves?"

"Yeah. Coach Kemp was diagnosed with prostate cancer. It's pretty bad, and he's fighting for his life. I've always wanted my own team, but not like this. It's been tough for us all."

"I'm sorry to hear that." Her voice holds sincerity, and then she offers a heart-thumping smile. "I hear you're really good, though."

A grin fights its way through the sobriety of the moments before. "I'm decent, I guess. They haven't fired me yet."

"Modest," she says. "I like it."

"Not really. Just self-aware."

We stop at a cream-colored Tesla Model X. She hits a button on her fob and the butterfly doors wing up.

"Holy shit." I'm not immune to the sexy lines of a car most only dream of.

"My indulgence." Pink dusts her high cheekbones, the only sign of self-consciousness in her otherwise sure movements while she loads her case into the car.

"You work hard," I tell her, loading my cases in the back seat beside hers. "You deserve to treat yourself."

"And I do. Believe me. I'm quite the diva."

"I don't buy that at all."

"Ask my best friend."

"Banner?"

"You know her?" she asks, then her brow clears. "Of course. She's the agent for some of your guys."

"Well, yeah, and you mentioned her in your story today."

"Oh, right." She pats the hood of the Tesla and turns a goodbye smile on me. "Well, I guess I'd better—"

"Would you like to grab coffee?" I blurt with the grace and subtlety of a rhinoceros.

She stares at me for a distended moment, wide green eyes clearly reflecting her surprise. Hell, she's a fitness mogul. She probably drinks kale or something.

"Or a smoothie," I offer. "There's a place around the corner where we could—"

"Maybe some other time," she says, a slight frown creasing her forehead. "I'm leaving on tour in a couple of days."

In a couple of days. Not today. But still not interested.

"I have a new book dropping Tuesday," she explains, which, even if it's true, feels like a kind way to let the awkward guy down.

"Ah," I murmur. It's a useless sound that doesn't tell her anything about how much I admire her strength. About how attracted I've been to her since the first time I saw her at the ESPYs a few years ago.

Yes, years. It's taken me this long to get up the nerve to approach this woman, and I'm failing miserably. Give me a clipboard, shitty odds and thirty seconds on the clock, and I'm your guy. One woman a foot shorter than me, and I apparently lose all my nerve.

"What's the name of your book?" My mush-for-brain manages to send a signal to my mouth to speak.

"*Bionic Beauty*," she says, her smile reappearing. "It chronicles a year consulting with fashion designers to create prosthetic art. One of the most awkward parts of this whole leg thing is how people stare, especially the parents who tell their kids *not* to stare, which silently communicates there's something wrong with us. Like we are something to be ashamed of and looked away from. I wanted to create something that makes it even harder to look away. Not because it's awkward and you pity the girl who lost a leg, but you can't look away because there's something so arresting there."

She doesn't need a book or a tour or fashion designers to do that for her. The passion on her face, the fire in her eyes while she talks, has me completely captivated.

"Well, I better go," she says.

For whatever reason, I press my hand to the small of her back when she turns to get in her car. Her body is lean and strong, but through the thin material of her dress, she feels soft, warm. I wish I could spread my fingers where her back curves in, caress the arch of it.

I'm creeping *myself* out, so I drop my hand. She doesn't seem to have even noticed.

She climbs in, settling into the peanut-butter-colored leather seats.

"If you change your mind about the coffee." I put my hand on the door before she can close it. "It's my off-season, so I have plenty of free time."

Lies.

I already canceled one meeting to see her today. In the off-season, I work nearly as much as I do when we're playing. Preparation proves itself.

"Look, that's sweet," she says, leaning back into the decadent leather and caressing the intricate stitching on her steering wheel. "But I'm really busy, and I honestly don't have time for . . . coffee. Coffee slows me down."

"Interesting effect when it seems to accelerate for most."

"Coffee isn't necessary," she goes on as if I haven't spoken. "Thanks for the help, but I need to go to my next appointment."

And in a flourish of outrageously expensive steel and electric car engineering, she's gone.

Chapter 2

Quinn

Men like him don't . . .

I won't finish that thought. That's how *she* used to think. That girl who wallowed in her own pain and depression, who assumed her life was over anyway, so why not just end it? I don't usually talk about my suicide attempts unless someone asks, but today I did. Did I do it subconsciously because I was so aware of Ean Jagger looming at the back of the room? Was I trying to scare him off? Or draw him in? Was it a test? If it was, I don't know if he passed or failed, but I know he kept on coming.

At first, I thought I imagined his stare—the fixed intensity of it that warmed me even in the air-conditioning. But as my talk went on, I was more aware of him than every other person in the room, even though he didn't say much. He's a hard man to ignore, though I don't think he realizes it. Obviously, there's his height. I'm five seven in bare feet. In my heels today I stood about five ten, and he still towered nearly a foot over me. I'd put him at around six seven. With that height, those black-rimmed glasses, and shoulders so wide they blocked the sun when he stood with me in the parking lot, he reminds me of Clark Kent. The obvious leashed power of that huge body and the austere beauty of his face make me want to see the S on his chest beneath that shirt. He's arresting, but not flashy like so many of the guys I meet in LA.

Over the years, it's become harder to discern men's motives when it comes to romance. When I was using a wheelchair and then a walker as I started the long process of re-learning mobility and regaining confidence, they weren't exactly knocking down my door. But I became America's Titanium Sweetheart and realized life wasn't about the leg I lost, but about the woman I found inside of me. She is resilient and tough and ambitious and generous.

She became really rich really fast.

And all of a sudden, boom. The men were back. I never know if it's my renewed confidence and the way I take care of this body that's been through so much, or if it's my fatter purse that's drawing them, so I take very few up on their offers.

Coffee.

That's what Ean offered today, but I couldn't bring myself to accept. I read so much more in his eyes than *coffee*. He searched my face, fixed on me like there wasn't anything else he wanted to see. Another man looked at me that way not long ago. Ted fooled me with those eyes that seemed to offer as much as they asked for, but he was a fraud. Ean Jagger seems like the real deal, but I don't have time for the hurt if he's not. I got shit to do.

That would be a great T-shirt in my QuinnPossible fitness line.

"I got shit to do," I say, pausing packing to voice record on my phone. "New T-shirt for QP."

I envisioned QP while out hiking. Banner had a proposal and possible investors lined up within the week. That girl is a badass, but then, so am I. We make a formidable team. There are always so many ideas passing through my head at any given time, I'd lose half of them if not captured immediately. And ideas are money.

My phone is still up to my mouth from voice recording when it starts ringing. I glance at the name on the screen and smile.

"What's up, Willa?" I ask.

"A helluva lot," my assistant answers, the coarse response at odds with the Marilyn Monroe breathiness of her voice. "How are you this morning?"

"Good." I fold my favorite silk pajamas and lay them in the suitcase. "Packing for this road trip."

"Great. Exactly why I was calling. Did you get your itinerary?"

"Yup. Car will be here at ten tomorrow morning? That right?"

"Yes, ma'am. And the deets for Atlanta and New York are in the email, too."

"I saw."

"And you end this leg of the trip in San Diego."

"Then a few days off the road before jumping back on. Got it."

"Smart of you to insist on that," she says.

"I know myself and I know my body." I run a hand over silky underwear no one other than me has seen in a long time. "I need just a few days in my house and in my life before I go back out there."

"The book is already getting great press."

"Yay," I auto-reply, mentally reviewing my checklist to make sure I'm not forgetting anything.

"Make sure you find time to actually *do* some fun stuff while you're on the road."

"You've seen my schedule. Exactly when will I find time for anything fun?"

"It can be simple. There's a famous ice cream shop called The Bent Spoon right across from the theater on Princeton's campus."

"Dairy." I shudder.

"You're not lactose intolerant. I know all your allergies. You're allergic to stupidity and meanness. That's about it."

"Don't forget douchery." I laugh and sit on the edge of my bed. "I'm highly allergic to that shit."

"A scoop of ice cream won't tie you up in knots. It's more the experience than anything else. Simple pleasures, Q."

Simple pleasures.

Like a man's big, warm hand at your back, leaving you feeling desired and cherished with something as simple as a touch.

But feelings like those are rarely simple.

Chapter 3

Ean

"D o I need to talk to Granger?" I ask Mack Decker, San Diego Waves' president of basketball operations. "We need this crap settled before the season starts. We can't afford another suspension."

"Maybe." He shrugs wide shoulders in his polo shirt. "He's one of Banner's guys, so she'll probably have the situation resolved before we have to intervene. She won't want the league involved either. Everyone knows she keeps her players in line."

She does, for sure. The only thing Banner might be *more* well-known for is her famous Titanium Sweetheart.

"What do you, um, know about Quinn Barrow?" I lean back in my seat at our favorite taco shop and take a sip of my beer.

Deck glances at me over a bite of his veggie-laden taco. They're one of his few cheats. I've never met anyone more disciplined with what goes into his body than Deck. It's a legacy from when he was a player himself, and part of why he's a future first round Hall of Famer.

"Quinn?" He wipes his mouth with a napkin and narrows his eyes at me. "You asking for you?"

I clench my teeth and sit up straight. I've never been one of those guys who talked about "conquests" with other men, or who asked for advice when it came to a woman I wanted. Even when I was a baller myself, I didn't take full advantage of the sexual perks that came with the sport. I'm more of a relationship guy, but I haven't had as many of those as most men my age. I don't like drama. I abhor messiness. And people are often both.

"Just asking," I grit out. "What can you tell me?"

Decker's wicked smile grates on my damn nerves.

"Jag likes a girl," he sing-songs.

"Fuck you, Deck." I tip my beer back for a quick swallow. "Never mind."

"Sorry, sorry." He holds his hands up and widens his grin. "This is a brand-new experience. I've known you since college, dude, and I can't remember you ever asking about a woman."

"Well, when I want to know something, I find out for myself, but Quinn . . . well, she's different."

"Because she's an amputee?" Deck frowns.

"What?" I glare at him. "Hell, no. Not because of that. If anything, because maybe she's out of my league."

Deck chokes on a chuckle and Dos Equis. "Out of your league? Dude, women love you."

I roll my eyes and grimace. "Whatever."

"You're just buried so deep in your Xs and Os, you don't notice."

Don't care is more like it. I have needs. Of course I do. And I satisfy them, like most guys, but I'm forty, not fourteen. Getting ass for the sake of it gets old.

Maybe it gets lonely and pointless after a while, too.

"They're into that moody, broody vibe you got going on," Decker elaborates unnecessarily. "Tall, dark, handsome. The glasses make 'em think you're smart. Hot nerd is a thing."

I snort. "I'm not a nerd."

"I beg to differ. Nobody generates the kind of data and stats and strategies that you do without having a significant amount of nerd in him."

"That's my job. I take it seriously."

"That's why we snapped you up as soon as possible." Deck takes another bite. "You're doing a damn good job leading the team, by the way."

"How's Coach Kemp?" I ask with a frown.

Deck puts his taco down and steeples his fingers, elbows resting on the table. He answers only with a grave shake of his head.

"Shit." I set my beer down, too. "He looked pretty bad when I went to see him a few weeks ago, but I'd hoped . . ."

"There's hope till there isn't," Deck says, twisting his lips and picking his taco back up. "But it only reiterates that life is too short not to go for something when you think it could be special." He angles a knowing look across the table. "When you think *she* could be special."

"How'd you know Avery was special?"

The satisfied grin that usually overtakes his face when someone mentions his wife is on full display. "Well, that's quite the story. The first time we met, she was trying to interview me in the locker room, and I dropped my towel."

"Damn." I chuckle, shaking my head. "Knowing Avery, I'm surprised she left your balls attached."

"Barely. She was spitting like a little cat, but there was also this buzz between us. Like a vibe I'd never felt with anyone before or since. Not even my ex-wife, I'm ashamed to say."

"Wait a minute. You were a player when you guys first met? But you've only been together a few years."

"Right." A shadow passes over his face. "We wasted ten years. I married my ex, and we had my daughter, who I wouldn't trade for anything. Avery got engaged to someone else. That we finally made it back to each other is a small miracle."

The look he aims at me is frank and knowing. "I don't advise leaving it to a miracle, if you don't have to," he says. "When I saw an opening with Avery, I did the full-court press, man."

"One-on-one defense," I say, nodding. "No letting up."

"You got it. So figure out your own strategy, but don't just sit around with your thumb up your ass. You know once the season kicks in, you won't have time to explore this properly. If you think

Quinn might be someone special, and there might be a connection, don't waste time asking me about her. Learn about her for yourself. And even more importantly, let *her* learn *you*."

I pull my phone from my pocket. The screen defaults to the website I've been checking compulsively since I met Quinn yesterday. Titaniumsweetheart.com shows a pic of Quinn, her hair slightly longer than it was yesterday, and wearing a T-shirt that reads "QuinnPossible." I click on the upcoming appearances tab, and a long list of cities and venues pops up.

Wow. I thought my life was busy. Deck's right. Once the season kicks in, I won't have time to pursue her in earnest. If I want to see if there's something worth pursuing with Quinn, I'll have to chase her. She may not be a world-class runner anymore, but looking at the appearances posted on her site for the next few months, she still moves fast. If I want to catch her, I'll have to go on the offensive. If this were a game, I'd tell my team to move the ball up the court and get into scoring position as quickly as possible.

"I think I have my strategy," I tell Decker, grinning and sipping the last of my beer.

"Oh yeah?" he asks. "What is it?"

"A fast break."

Chapter 4

Quinn

"I know most people look at me and see what I've lost." I tap my left leg, tonight brushed metal carbon studded with rhinestones down the side. "And I get it. That's how I felt at first, too. But now, I see what I've gained."

I pause and look over the packed audience at Princeton's McCarter Theatre Center. "It wasn't the circumstances that changed my life so radically for good," I say. "It's what I chose to do with them. How I chose to see them. As a runner, maybe I would have qualified for the Olympics. Ended up on a box of Wheaties, sure. And done some great stuff, but losing my leg, and going through the hell of accepting my new reality, of learning to walk and run again. Learning to live again and even better than before—that transformed my trajectory."

I gesture to all of them. "I wouldn't be here with you tonight. Without adversity, I wouldn't have written books on overcoming it. There wouldn't be a gym called Titanium because there would be no Titanium Sweetheart."

I smile when the audience laughs.

"The leg I'm wearing tonight and so many like it might not exist because I wouldn't have been passionate about elevating disability through art and fashion," I say, holding up my book *Bionic Beauty*. "I gave folks something beautiful to look at when they stare. Without this, maybe I would be living a good life, but I wouldn't be living *this* life. And I love this one. I wouldn't trade it for anything. Thank you."

The applause is most gratifying because it signals the event is almost over. I love what I do, but after flight delays and the preparation for tonight, I'm ready to be done.

"Ms. Barrow has graciously agreed to answer some of our questions," the moderator, one of the students who coordinated bringing me here, says. "We'll take just a few, and we have mics set up in the aisles."

I've been standing almost a solid hour and after a long flight, my neck and shoulders feel tight. The muscles in my legs ache. I sit gratefully on the high stool and take a sip of water.

Over the next fifteen minutes, I field questions. The usual. Do I have phantom pain? How does it feel to walk with a prosthetic? What about showering?

The moderator walks to the edge of the stage. "I think that's all we have time—"

"Sorry," a deep voice interrupts from one of the aisle mics. "I have one last question."

I glance up sharply, recognizing the deep rumble of that voice. But it couldn't be him. Why would he be . . .?

"Ms. Barrow," Ean Jagger says, squatting because the mic won't pull up far enough to reach his mouth. "My question was of a more personal nature."

Women and a few men around him study him closely, whispering behind their hands. Some may recognize him. Some may just be admiring what is, I must admit, a fine specimen of a man.

"How personal?" I ask, managing a teasing smile, partly to put the audience at ease and partly to demonstrate to him that I'm not easily flustered, even when ambushed in front of a crowd.

A white smile is a flash of brilliance against his tan, which is part California sun, part genetics.

"With such a demanding schedule," he says, "is it hard to find time for personal relationships?"

"Personal relationships?" I ask, crinkling my expression into a small frown. "Of what nature exactly?"

A murmur of interest ripples through the audience. I'm not that chick who gets bothered with attention, but even meeting him only once, I know he is not a spotlight guy. Let's see what he does with it.

"Well, I guess of a . . ." He meets my gaze boldly, and even with the length of the theater separating us, I feel the impact of those dark, intense eyes shielded by his glasses but so exposed. ". . . of a romantic nature."

The mumbling of the audience grows louder, punctuated by clearing throats and giggling.

"Be more specific," I command, standing and slipping my hands into the pockets of my pencil skirt.

"Dates," he fires back, never dropping his glance from my face. "With your schedule so full, do you make time for dates?"

"Are you asking for a friend?"

The audience outright laughs at my retort, and a muscle along the side of his jaw tightens and flexes. He doesn't smile.

"No, I'm asking for myself," he says, the serious note in his voice squelching the crowd's amusement to low murmurs that peter out while they wait for my response. "Would you have dinner with me?"

"No."

I let the word land in the room, and feel the tension and the embarrassment on his behalf, the awkwardness on mine. I let us all live in the tighter walls and cloying air of our collective discomfort for a moment before I go on.

"But how do you feel about ice cream?"

Chapter 5

Ean

I still can't believe I did that.

The guy who avoids cameras as much as possible, and who leaves the spotlight to my players whenever I can. The one who finds relief in being the coach and garnering less attention than star athletes.

I still can't believe she said yes.

Well, sort of.

"So you like ice cream?" I ask, filling the quiet of our first steps from the theater through Princeton's Palmer Square.

"Not much." She glances up at me, eyes gleaming emerald in the golden light of the lamps lining the college town's sidewalks. "My assistant told me about this place and said to make sure I check it out."

This place turns out to be The Bent Spoon. There's a short line spilling beyond the entrance, and a wooden bench beneath the large square window providing glimpses into the charming space.

"It's famous for the unusual flavors," she tells me.

I nod, unsure of how to proceed. I didn't think this through very well. Fly to Princeton. Ask her on a date . . . in front of five hundred people. Hold my breath and brace for complete humiliation.

Possible outcomes from there:

1. Hit a bar and drown sorrows in the hardest liquor I could find.
2. Jump on a plane and drag my ass home.
3. Have dinner with the most amazing woman I've ever met.

This isn't exactly any of those, but it's close enough to number three for me to feel like this was a good call.

"So you do this often?" she asks while we wait in the short line for the ice cream shop.

"Do I do what often?" I ask, deliberately playing dumb so she can articulate exactly how she views my actions. Stalking? Grand romantic gesture? Kamikaze mission?

"Oh, you know. Ambush women in the middle of public speaking engagements so they'll go out with you."

I smile, but it kind of hurts to force it. "Is this a pity date then? You didn't want to make me look bad?

"Surely you calculated that as part of the equation." Her dark brown brows disappear under a fringe of ginger hair falling into her face. "I'm not the only one who's famous. Many of those people know you better than they know me."

"I didn't mean to manipulate you." I clear my throat, feeling like an idiot. "Thank you for trying to spare my feelings. You didn't have to." I step out of line and back away.

"Don't feel like you have to do this." I gesture toward the ice cream shop. "I'm sure you're tired. I could walk you to your hotel if you want. Or not. If you want to be alone, I can—"

"I get a lot of time alone," she says, looking at me steadily. "I have a lot of miles ahead of me for the next few months. I don't mind some company tonight."

She tips her head toward The Bent Spoon. "Besides, I want to try their farm-fresh ricotta."

"Ricotta ice cream?" I ask, skeptical, and step back in line with her.

"I told you they have unusual flavors. My assistant sent the menu."

She pulls it up on her phone and I bend to see. That clean, citrusy scent wraps around me, and I sneak a breathful of her.

"You're like really tall," she says softly.

I glance down at her and grin. "Occupational hazard."

"Not all coaches are tall."

"I was a baller first." I shrug. "I thought when I entered the NBA it would be on the court, not from the sidelines. I blew out my knee in college, and there went my hoops dreams."

"I can relate," she says wryly. "Life gives us limes, but we can make margaritas, is what I always say."

I chuckle, shuffling forward as the line moves. "I could have used an endless supply of those when I was in the hospital. All they gave me was Jell-O."

"Well, we have that in common then," she says, her smile dimming. "We both had to rethink our lives. Figure out a plan B."

"Yeah, but I think this is how it was always supposed to be. Strategy, statistics, leadership—those things are so much a part of me, and I think coaching is the best thing that could have happened. Not sure I would have seen that so early or so clearly if I'd had years in the league."

"Same. I meant what I said tonight. I love my life now. There have been obstacles to get here, and sometimes it's still tough, but you work for something when it's worth having."

"Agreed."

"I endured months of painful rehab, badly fitted prosthetics, the mental agony of letting that old girl go and figuring out who the new me really is, but the new me is pretty great."

"Agreed," I repeat, smiling down at her upturned face with the dewy skin and fine brows and long lashes.

We finally enter the ice cream shop, and I press my hand to the small of her back, urging her forward. She stiffens. I feel the line of tension in the delicate curve of it.

Damn. Am I that much of a creeper?

"Sorry," I murmur, dropping my hand.

"Why are you apologizing?" she asks, fixing her stare to the chalkboard menu with the flavor options.

"I didn't want you to think I was being intense, touching you when you don't want me to."

She slides her glance away from the menu to give me a wry look. "You fly all the way from Cali to Princeton, ask me out in front of hundreds of people, and you think a casual touch will come off as intense?"

We both laugh at how ridiculous that sounds. It's our turn to order, but before we start, I tell her the truth, hoping she continues to be freakishly okay with my odd behavior. "It doesn't feel casual to me."

Her green eyes zip to meet mine. Before she can respond, the young woman behind the counter gives us a friendly smile and asks a question that shelves Quinn's response for later.

"What'll you have?"

Chapter 6

Quinn

"How's your cheesy ice cream?" Ean asks.

I giggle, scoop out a spoonful of my farm-fresh ricotta ice cream and settle back into our bench on the square.

"Shockingly delicious," I say, laughing and thrusting my spoon at him. "Taste."

"Nah." He tips his head away and grins. "I'm fine with my dark chocolate."

"All those exotic flavors to choose from, and you played it safe."

"I think I've taken enough risks for one night," he says, his voice dry and his smile tipped to one side.

I watch him from the corner of my eye. His legs are a long, steely stretch of muscle. The tanned skin of his arms gleams with health, contrasting to the lemon-colored shirt. With him leaned back on the bench, the shirt clings to the ridged abdominal muscles. I roll the cool sweetness of my ice cream on my tongue. How does he taste at this very moment? The dark chocolate coating the lining of his jaw and those full lips.

He glances up and catches me looking at him. I wonder if something in my face alerts him to my thoughts, or at least that

I'm enjoying him. He goes still for a second, searching my eyes in that penetrative way. That way that feels like he's seeing inside me.

I scrape the sides of my paper cup and hold up the spoon. "All done."

He takes the last bite of his ice cream cone and dusts crumbs from his well-tailored pants. "Me, too."

We watch each other in our cocoon of silence while summer traffic flows around us, all polo shirts and sundresses. A palette of bright colors in the dim light from the moon and street lamps.

"I have an early flight," I say, dropping my glance from his dark eyes to the firm, sensual curve of his mouth.

"Yeah, me, too." He licks his lips and clears his throat, standing to his feet.

"I'm at the Nassau Inn," I say once we start walking. I tip my head toward the hotel with its cedar clapboard shingles.

"Yeah, me, too."

We walk so close, still silent, and our hands keep brushing. The fourth time it happens, he links our fingers and tugs me closer. Unabashedly, I huddle beneath the muscled bulk of him, feeling protected.

And terribly horny.

"I'm on the second floor," I say.

"Yeah, me, too."

We laugh at his continued use of that phrase, and take the stairs. Once we reach my room, I turn to face him, pressing my back to the door. I don't want the night to end—don't want *this* to end. Need and want tangle inside me, building from my core and spreading perilously close to my heart. It's been over a year since I slept with a man. My last experience wasn't exactly reassuring when it comes to the male species. Between the frenetic pace of my life and the doubt Ted planted in my head, intimacy, physical and otherwise, hasn't been high on my list of priorities. But tonight, it is. With Ean it is.

"You could come in if you like." My voice is husky, raw with the desire I'm sure he can read in my eyes, and in the way I can't stop scouring his broad, beautiful body or the stark planes of his handsome face.

"I'm not sure that's a good idea," he says, a slight frown pulling his dark brows together.

My chest deflates, a balloon pricked by irritation.

Seriously?

Who flies across the country to ask a woman on a date so publicly, *so damn romantically*, and doesn't want to get laid when the opportunity presents itself tied up with a bow at the end of the night?

Unless . . .

Maybe he's not sure how it will be with me? It's easy to forget what I'm "missing" when I'm up and about, so capable and all confident on stage. When the bedroom doors close, the clothes aren't the only things that come off.

"It's fine." I nod jerkily. "I get it."

I didn't expect it from Ean somehow, but after my last experience with a guy I thought I knew, I shouldn't be surprised. I really have to stop trusting my instincts if they're going to keep leading to a dented heart. Not broken. I refuse to have anything on my body break for anyone.

"What do you think you get, Quinn?" he asks, the slight frown deepening, his expression darkening.

"I thought . . . it's fine," I say hastily, just wanting to get out of the hall and into my room away from him. "Some men aren't sure how it'll be. You aren't the first to think you could handle it and then—"

He pulls me up against his chest, cutting off my words. His mouth on mine is a brand, a possession of hot silk and sweet, dark chocolate. The taste of him explodes on my tongue and I push up on my toes, widening my mouth under his. He strokes down my back, those wide hands that first stirred sensation between us with a single touch fitting to my hips. He groans against my mouth.

"Fuck, Quinn," he says, dragging his lips down the curve of my neck. "How could you think I don't want this? I'm burning up with it."

I reach between us to find him, grasping the huge erection that tells me he's not lying. He's so thick between my fingers. My panties are soaked at the thought of him stretching me.

"Then stay." I roll a hand over the tightly muscled curve of his ass, jerking him closer. "I want it, too."

He delves deeper into my mouth, his tongue hunting for mine, tangling with mine urgently. He takes his time tasting me and slides his hand lower to cup my butt. He pulls me up until his dick slots between my legs. I moan at the sensation and grind into him.

"Hell, yes." I kiss him back, harder, deeper. This is gonna happen. I imagine this towering man slamming into my much smaller body, hovering over me and spreading my legs. My mouth waters. I want to suck his dick. I want to stick my finger in his ass. I want to do all the things I haven't done with or to anyone in a year, but I want them with him. I haven't missed dick as much as I thought I would during this drought, but all of a sudden, I'm so damn thirsty.

He breaks our kiss, pulling me up higher on my toes until foreheads touch. "I'm going to my room, Quinn."

My eyes snap open, shock immobilizing me. "You're what? Going where?"

"To my room." With gentle fingers, he pushes the bangs back from my face. "You're so beautiful."

"Gee, thanks, but I don't want compliments. I want to fuck. With you. Tonight." I point my thumb over my shoulder toward my room. "Preferably in there, but I'm so worked up I'm not opposed to putting on a show right here in the hall."

He smiles, lowers his head for a whisper of a kiss across my lips. "I'm glad you want this, too. That makes me feel like less of an idiot for flying here."

"You came all this way," I say, my tone wheedling. "Don't you want to just—"

"I want more than a quick fuck, Quinn," he says, his smile fading and his voice firming. "Our first night has been great. There's time for more."

"But . . ."

He reaches into my skirt pocket and pulls my phone out, punching numbers in and sending a text.

"Now you have my number," he says. "And I have yours. We'll stay in touch."

In *touch?* I want to stay in touch all right. I want to touch him from the top of that wavy hair to the tips of his big feet, which I hope portend a huge dick that I can barely accommodate.

But apparently I won't find out tonight. If I was irritated before, I'm downright mad now. Sexually frustrated. And a little humiliated.

"Whatever," I say, fumbling with my room key and hurrying inside. "Good night."

I close the door before he can say another word.

Chapter 7

Ean

I landed in Atlanta late.

Not my fault. Damn airline. Delayed flights. I planned to make it in time to hear Quinn speak at Emory University, but when my car pulls up to Glenn Memorial Auditorium, the crowd has dispersed and Quinn's nowhere in sight.

"Dammit."

This is what I get for chasing a woman across the country . . . again. Especially when she hasn't returned my texts or calls. I've only sent a few over the last couple of days since we saw each other, but I've had no response. I hope I properly conveyed how wrong she was to assume me not spending the night wasn't about me not wanting her. Nothing could be further from the truth. I jerked off in the shower as soon as I reached my hotel room. And try flying four hours with your dick as hard as a brick. It happens every time I remember that kiss, and not just the heat of it.

But the warmth.

The sense of rightness from the moment our lips touched until I had to drag my mouth away, acutely aware that I was mere seconds from fucking America's Titanium Sweetheart up against the door in a hall for anyone to see.

My gut tells me there's something that needs repairing. Not just from our encounter the other night, but something in *her* that needs mending. I don't have any illusions I can fix it, fix her, but I could at least soothe. If she'll let me. If she'll talk to me.

"Gimme a second," I say to the car service driver I asked to wait until I knew if Quinn were still here.

My finger is poised to press Quinn's contact to call her, when my phone flashes an Instagram notification. I set it to alert me when Quinn makes a post. There's a photo of her and Banner.

@QuinnPossible When your girl #BannerMorales surprises you on the road! Thank you for having me tonight @emmoryuniversity! I'm loving ATL. Now to get our grub on. I've heard good things about @sluttyveganatl! I'll report back!

"Hey," I say, catching the driver's glance in the rearview mirror. "Take me to the Slutty Vegan."

Chapter 8

Quinn

"Dios," Banner mutters around a sloppy bite of her burger. "Are we sure there's no meat in this?"

"That's what they say." I laugh and sink my teeth into my own. "But that can't be right. Nothing vegan can taste this guilty."

"What's yours called?"

"I got the Super Slut." I giggle and lift the top bun away. "Let's see. We got guac, jalapeños, vegan cheese, caramelized onions and that slutty sauce they use. What's yours?"

"The Sloppy Toppy." She shakes her head before taking another bite. "I'm gonna regret this next week. I'm tempted not to log this meal in my *Girl, You Better* app. I don't want my balls busted over my caloric intake."

"I didn't design it to make you feel bad, and hey. At least it's vegan."

Banner lifts a skeptical brow and swipes at the slutty sauce dripping down her chin. "I'll work out extra hard tomorrow. That new trainer isn't quite the slave driver you are."

"All the more reason for me to wrap this tour up soon so I can get back in the gym. My clients need me." I train a handful of people, Banner being one of them.

"Aren't you enjoying being in a different city every night, sharing your pearls of wisdom with sold-out crowds?" Banner teases. "Having your adoring public fawning all over you?"

I'd settle for one man to "fawn" all over me, but I've been ignoring him. I'm not even sure why. The embarrassment of his rejection faded before I fell asleep *alone* in my bed. It's something else holding me back. Something I don't want to address, but will have to soon enough.

"Thanks for coming, B," I tell my best friend.

From day one, we were more than agent and client. She came to my hospital bed with nothing but compassion. She was barely out of college herself at the time, but she convinced me to give life another chance.

"I wanted to make it to the first stop at Princeton," she says. "But both my babies made that impossible."

"Both?" I ask, pausing with the burger halfway to my mouth. "You keeping something from me? I thought I only had the one niece."

"Angela is easy compared to the other baby in my house." She pauses to give me a wry look. "Jared."

I chuckle and shake my head. Banner's husband is the classic alpha male—possessive, territorial, and hates being away from his wife.

"I'm literally taking the red-eye to get home before daybreak," she says, affecting an aggrieved tone.

"You don't fool me. I know you want to be home with him as badly as he wants you there."

Her broad smile is beautiful to behold. "Yeah, you're right. I get so homesick being away from him and Angela. I don't want to miss a thing with them. Can you believe I'm already done breast-feeding?" She blinks at sudden tears. "My milk is all dried up now."

"Guess you'll just have to have another one," I tease gently.

"You know I'm ready. It's Jared who has to be convinced."

They've only been married a few years, but if it was up to Banner, they'd be on their way to a house full of babies.

"He can't deny you anything. He'll give you a dozen kids if you want."

"Oh, I want." She slides a glance over to me. "And what about you? I haven't heard you talk about anyone since Ted."

Ugh. Even hearing his name . . .

"And we both know how that turned out," I mumble, setting my burger down as my appetite disappears.

"Hey, he was a jerk."

"One I didn't see through until it was almost too late."

"There will be someone else," Banner says, her voice gentle.

"There, um . . . maybe there is a prospect," I admit, unsure if I want to discuss this with Banner. She'll dig, and I'm not about that tonight.

"Who?" she demands, her eyes wide and her virtual antennae piqued. "How could you not tell me?"

"It's not anything official. One kiss does not—"

"A kiss?" Banner whisper-shouts. "Tell me, bitch. You've been holding out."

"It's nothing. Ean Jagger just—"

"*Coach* Jagger?" Banner squeaks. "Like, the coach of the San Diego Waves Ean Jagger?"

"Um, yeah."

"And you didn't tell me?"

"I'm trying to tell you now, but you keep interrupting."

"Okay. That's fair. Now tell me everything."

I recount meeting him at August's summer camp. The flare of attraction. Him showing up at Princeton and asking me out on a date in front of the crowd. By the time I get to the kiss, Banner's eyes and mouth are both wide open.

"Are you freaking kidding me?" Banner shakes her head like she's dazed. "But he . . . he barely speaks. He's downright . . . curt. They call him The Machine because he has a photographic court memory."

"I can attest that he is definitely flesh and blood."

And bone.

God, the thick, rigid length of him in my hand. Those broad shoulders, the tapered waist, and that ass. I squirm in my seat, hot and wet between my legs.

"I made it very clear I was . . . open," I admit, my face heating in a rare blush. "But he turned me down. Said he wanted more than a quick fuck."

"And it's bad that a brilliant, handsome, wealthy, successful man like Ean Jagger wants more than one night with you? Maybe wants to build something meaningful?"

I shrug, not wanting to examine my feelings too closely.

"If this is about that slimeball Ted—"

"It's not." I hold her stare to convince her. "It's not about him. I just think if Ean's looking for more than one night and a good time, maybe I'm not the one for him."

"Well," Banner says, grinning at something over my shoulder, "I think it'll be more than one night. Forget what I said about The Machine. He's a fucking dreamboat."

"Huh?"

I look over my shoulder and almost drop my Impossible burger when I see six feet and seven inches of determined, fine-ass male headed toward our table.

Chapter 9

Ean

Good thing I came straight here, or I might not have caught her.

Caught her being the operative phrase. There's no denying you're chasing a woman when you fly across the country twice in a week to see her. When you ignore *her* ignoring *you* and come anyway.

"Quinn, hey," I say when I reach her table. I nod to Banner. "Ms. Morales-Foster, good to see you."

"Good to see you, too, Coach." She darts a look between Quinn and me, her lips pulling into a smile.

A silence settles around us, and Quinn is still watching me, but hasn't spoken.

"I hope your boy Granger shapes up before the season starts," I address Banner again, since Quinn is officially mute in this conversation.

"He'll get his shit together," she says. "I promise I'll have him there first day of training camp, ready to earn his keep."

I nod and smile the slightest bit. "Good to hear."

"Well, I've got a plane to catch," Banner says, checking the time on her phone.

"Already?" Quinn asks, glaring at her friend. "I thought it was a red-eye."

"Still gotta swing by the hotel to get my luggage." She taps her screen a few times. "Grabbing an Uber."

"I have the driver here waiting," Quinn protests with a frown.

"Great. When you're ready to leave," Banner says, standing, "he'll take you wherever you want to go."

"Banner—"

"Love you," Banner cuts in over Quinn and reaches down for a hug. She turns a blinding smile on me. "Good to see you, Coach. I'll keep you and the front office apprised of Granger's progress."

"Thanks," I murmur. "Safe trip home."

With one last pointed look at Quinn, she heads toward the door.

"Can I sit?" I ask.

"Here?" Quinn lifts her brows and firms the lush line of her mouth. "Are you sure? Wouldn't want to take things too fast."

I blow out a breath, half amused, half exasperated. "You're not going to make me feel guilty for not wanting to sleep with you on the first date. Surely that's some kind of double standard."

She shrugs, her bare shoulders smooth and lightly tanned. The bodice of her dress hugs the high curve of her breasts. Her hair, finger-tousled, bright and coppery like a new penny, glints under the restaurant's lights. "Sit if you want to."

I pull up a seat and lean back, watching her until she looks up and watches me back.

"Why are you upset with me?" I ask after another few moments of quiet.

"No one wants to be left hanging and horny, Coach." She twists her lips to a wry angle. "I guess I was confused. I thought I knew what you were about. I must have miscalculated."

"What did you think I wanted? I'm pretty sure we want the same thing, but I just wanted to wait for it a little longer."

"I assumed you were just a stump humper." She gives another of those careless shrugs of her pretty shoulders that are driving me crazy.

"What the hell is a stump humper?" I ask, mildly irritated by how things are *not* going as I hoped.

"Someone who gets off on fucking amputees," she says, lifting her eyes to mine with deliberate provocation.

I go still and grind my teeth.

"I don't deserve that," I say softly. "I felt a connection with you from the moment we met. Hell, before we met."

I jerk my phone from my pocket and flip through the app icons until I reach *Girl, You Better*. "I downloaded this when it was in fucking *beta*. I've read both your books. Joined your gym in LA when I live in San Diego on the off chance that when I'm in town and work out there, I'd see you."

I stab a finger against the table to punctuate my point. "I've put myself out there with you not once, not twice, but three times now, risking a helluva lot to see where this could go."

I glare at her, unmoved when I see her eyes widen with every word I say. "And you dare to accuse me of something that vile? That twisted? When what I feel for you is . . ."

Pure.

I let the word melt in my mouth. I won't give her that. If she can't see what a chance with her would mean to me, how much I admire her, how much I want her for who she is and what we might be together, then fuck it.

I stand and cross the room, tapping my phone to select an Uber as I go. The Atlanta summer air slaps me across the face like a scorned lover—ironic, since I'm the one who feels wronged. The door opens behind me, leaking the sounds of laughing diners and Dirty South hip-hop.

"Cancel your Uber," she says.

I glance down and our gazes collide. I steel myself against going soft at those leaf-green eyes, and the resilience and strength behind them.

"I've got a car." She tips her head toward a dark SUV in the parking lot. "I can take you wherever you want to go. It's the least I can do."

"You mean the least you can do after being a brat and insulting me unfairly when all I wanted to do was get to know you better? To respect you?"

She drops her gaze to the ground and purses her lips before nodding. "Pretty much that, yeah."

For a moment, I don't move—I barely breathe. Huffing a frustrated breath, I cancel my Uber.

"Let's go." I don't wait for her, but start toward the SUV she indicated. I climb into the back seat and lean on the door, propping my elbow against the window.

"Where are you staying?" she asks.

`Shit.

"I don't exactly have a hotel yet," I mumble.

"What? You came all the way from San Diego without getting a place to stay?"

"It was a last-minute decision."

The only sound for the next few moments is the low growl of the vehicle's idling engine, the whoosh of air-conditioning, and Anita Baker's "Sweet Love" playing faintly through the sound system.

"I'm glad you came." She says it so softly I think I imagined it at first.

I turn to look at her, every flash of streetlight revealing the confusion in her eyes, on her face. "Didn't seem like it." I hold on to my hardness, trying my damnedest not to give in to the sway she holds over me.

"I'm sorry I ignored your calls and messages this week." She blows out a long breath. "I did act like a brat, and you're right. You didn't deserve it."

I turn on the seat and lean my back against the door so I can see her fully. "Why?"

She shrugs, drops her eyes to the seat between us. "I don't know. I—"

"Don't lie to me, Quinn." I reach over and tip her chin up with my index finger. "Why?"

She looks at me unblinkingly for a few seconds and bites her lip. "There's this guy."

My hand drops from her face and my back goes rigid. I hadn't expected that. Foolish of me. She's gorgeous and successful and smart. Of course *there's this guy.* She probably has a revolving door for all the men who want to be with her. Some random coach she doesn't even know starts showing up, but she has her pick of men, and I went too deep, too fast. Tried to make it something she isn't looking for.

"Whatever you're thinking right now with that scowl on your face," she says with a wry smile, "is probably wrong."

I nod. My thoughts *were* running a little wild there for a second. "Tell me."

She smooths the silky material of her skirt, and I notice she's wearing her "pretty shoes" leg and heels.

"There was this guy about a year or so ago," she says, "who started coming around. I met him at some industry party my publisher was throwing. He was handsome and had a great sense of humor. We had incredible conversations. I was attracted to him. We dated for a few weeks, and I was ready to take it to the next level."

I hate everything about this conversation, especially wherever it's headed because, based on the look on her face, it can't be anywhere good.

"I went to his house for dinner one night, and I was determined to show him I was ready to . . ." She dips her head and raises her brows. ". . . you know."

To fuck.

I hope she doesn't say it, because the thought of her, so sweet and sexy and strong, giving herself to someone who obviously proved unworthy somewhere along the way, makes me sick.

"I packed an overnight bag and everything." She laughs bitterly. "We were kissing and I told him I wanted to get comfortable—that I wanted to change."

She glances up self-consciously. "When you've worn the sock on your residual limb, there's a silicone liner, and after sweating all day . . . well, you just don't always feel fresh." She grimaces. "Not smelly, but I'm fastidious about cleaning it and showering before I go to bed even when I sleep alone. Sleeping with someone else . . . well I definitely prefer showering beforehand, especially the first time."

She glances down at her lap and draws in a deep breath before going on. "I came back into the house and didn't see him, so I wandered down the hall. I could hear him whispering in his bedroom about not being sure he could put me off any longer. That I wanted it so badly and was probably hard up because I hadn't had sex in so long. He called her 'baby,' and told her it would be worth it when I invested in his new product. That he wasn't going to fuck me because he wanted to, but for their future."

She laughs humorlessly. "Turns out he had a patent for a new resistance band. I guess I was some kind of sexual shark tank."

"I hope you slapped his fucking face," I grit out, my hands curled into fists at my side on the seat.

"I confronted him, yeah," she says, smiling. "But no slapping. I just told him to stay away from me and promised I would put the word out on the street that he was trash and into bestiality."

"Damn." I whistle. "Harsh, but I hope you took out an ad in the *LA Times*."

"I actually did something I hadn't done in a really long time." She twists her fingers in her lap, a bitter laugh cracking over her lips. "I cried."

"You cried?" I ask. "For that motherfucker?"

"No." She raises her eyes to meet mine in the dim interior light of the car. "For me, Ean. I cried for me."

Chapter 10

Quinn

I shake my head helplessly, not really completely understanding the emotion, the response myself. "I probably need to sort this out with my therapist," I say, forcing a laugh and not fooling either of us. "It's hard to articulate."

"Try." He reaches across the seat that separates us and takes my hand. For the first time since he walked into the restaurant, I relax. Maybe it will be okay. Maybe I haven't ruined it.

"It took me a long time to find the strength to do what I do," I say. "And I don't mean my career. I mean getting up in the morning. Looking in the mirror and accepting what I saw, just as it was. New reality and all."

I go silent and he squeezes my hand, signaling for me to go on.

"When you first start walking with a prosthetic," I say, "part of the process is learning to believe it will support you. That it will hold up under you. It takes a kind of faith. When you lose your leg, your whole center of balance is thrown off. I had the worst fear of falling when I first started, especially in public. The worst part was the pitying glances, or worse, the deliberate not looking. Ignoring you because of how uncomfortable it made *them*. I felt those not-stares much more deeply than the long, rude looks because those declared me invisible."

I swallow and go on, deliberately keeping my eyes averted. "Even after I was confident enough to become a public speaker and had run my first marathon, had done all these things I never thought I would again, I still had not been on a date."

His fingers tighten around mine, and I hazard a glance up before looking away again.

"I knew I was a badass," I say with a self-deprecating chuckle. "I knew I was smart and a good speaker and a great business-woman, but it took a long time for me to also see myself as desir-able. As *whole*, even though my leg was gone, but I did it. And I started dating, and being intimate with people I respected and who respected me. Sometimes I felt awkward, but I never felt unwanted. That's not because there aren't guys out there who will make you feel that way, because there are. I was careful not to let those guys into my life. I trusted myself to choose wisely. And then I didn't."

I shake my head and swallow my emotion. "I chose the wrong guy to want," I say, pouring all the self-censure I felt into the look I give Ean. "I allowed someone to infiltrate the world I had made for myself where I was fierce and confident and exactly who I was supposed to be. I allowed him to make me feel unwanted. Un-whole." I lower my head and bite my lip. "I haven't tried again since."

"You haven't been . . . *with* anyone in a year?"

"Right." I lift my lashes to catch his eyes on me, tender and warm. "It was like when I first started using the prosthetic. I didn't trust it to hold me and I was afraid to fall, but now I'm realizing falling is part of this life. We don't want to fall because we're afraid to get hurt, but sometimes the most human thing we can do is hurt, and the bravest thing we can do is heal. I forgot that over the last year."

"Why me?" he asks, and he's not fishing for compliments about how gorgeous he is in all his broody glory. Genuine curiosity flavors the query.

"Gosh, I don't know." I shrug through the lie. "I felt a connection to you at the basketball camp when you . . . you touched me on my—"

"Back. I touched your back and was sure you thought me a creeper, touching you like that."

"No. I thought how good it felt to be touched, actually. To be touched by a man who I believed wanted me for me. You asked me for coffee, but I could tell you wanted more."

"I wanted too much," he mutters.

"You know what I've figured out on my journey?" I ask softly. "Sometimes it's good to want too much. Sometimes wanting 'too much' is how we get it all."

A flare of feeling—emotion, desire, something deep and dark and tucked away—shows in his eyes. "Are you saying I should go after what I want?"

I nod tentatively, simultaneously excited, uncertain and turned on by the intensity of his stare.

"Okay," he says, pressing the button to lock the partition separating us from the driver. "I will."

Chapter 11

Ean

T he tiny *click* of the partition locking into place is the only sound in the back seat for a second, but Quinn's quick little stutter breaths fill the air. When our glances tangle in the dim light, it's like the sparks when kindling ignites. Sharp and quick and bright. I reach for her hand again and bring it to my lips. Without looking away from her face, I press my mouth to her palm and then scatter kisses between her fingers, spraying kisses over her wrist like perfume. I make my way up her arm, licking at the sensitive skin inside her elbow, and feel a shudder tremble through her slim body.

I rub my thumb over her nipple and watch it bead beneath the silk of her strapless dress. Her head tips back and she lies against the seat, exactly as I want her. My kisses wander from the delicate vellum skin behind her ear, across her stubborn chin and up to those pouty lips. It's a plunging kiss, sweeping the sweet, silky interior of her mouth with my tongue. I suck her bottom lip hard between mine, and then softening to tiny bites. I shove my hand into the short cap of her curls, relishing the way the silky strands cling to my fingers.

"I want to suck your breasts," I whisper against her lips. "Can I?"

Her chest heaves with a deep breath and she nods. "Yeah. Okay."

I slip my mouth down her neck, dragging that clean, citrus scent in and kissing her collarbone. I edge the dress's neckline with my lips, teasing her with the promise of my mouth on her nipples. She shifts, her hips circling, and I hear little whimpers escaping her throat.

That's it, baby. I want you to want this until it drives you as crazy as I've become.

I open my mouth over one nipple through the dress, dampening the silk with the hard suction of my mouth.

"Shit," she mutters, arching her back, pressing her nipple deeper into my mouth. "Jag, come on."

Damn, that's sexy. She's never called me that before, and I'm determined she'll scream my name just like that before the night is over. I'll save fucking her for the hotel. For now, I just want her to come all over this nice man's leather seats.

I keep mouthing her and sliding my hand up her thigh, the skin so smooth and firm. I run a finger over the silk covering her pussy.

"God," I groan, pressing my knuckle against her clit. "You're dripping. I can't wait to taste you."

She moans and twists, jerking the strapless dress down to expose her breasts. I stop and stare. They're full and firm with candy-coated nipples my mouth is on before I think to ask again.

"Yes." She breathes her pleasure and I lower my head over her. She drives her fingers into my hair, pushing, filling my mouth with the sweet, soft flesh. I move my mouth from one to the other, loving the taste, the feel of them both, until she's panting and begging, spreading her legs in subtle, brazen invitation.

"I love that you know what you want," I tell her, my hand traveling down the bare skin between her breasts, over her stomach, under her dress and between her thighs. I slip my fingers into her panties and rub the pads of my fingers across her clit. She jerks, her hips lifting. I start again, roughening my touch the longer I go until

I'm pinching and twisting the small knot of nerves. The sound of her wetness sets my blood on fire. She moans, biting her lip and reaching up to grab her own breast, tweaking the nipple. I slide down to the floor. I'm a big guy and it's a tight space, but I only need room for two things. My mouth and her pussy.

I peel her panties down over her legs, being careful when I reach the prosthetic. I don't want to hurt her and I'm not sure if anything I do will.

"You're fine," she says, her smile tentative, and yet sure. "It doesn't hurt."

I nod and lift her legs over my shoulders. With no dress and no panties cloaking her, the scent of her arousal is thick and all around me. It makes me groan. I don't know how I'm going to make it out of here alive. I brush the side of my nose over the skin inside her thighs, letting her get accustomed to me, to having me so near her most secret, intimate place. Once her thighs quiver against my cheeks, I push in deeper, swiping between the damp, plump lips with my tongue.

"Oh," she says, sending the one word to the next octave.

I do it again, a longer swipe. A more deliberate pressure of my tongue against her clit. Her fingers tighten in my hair, urging me on. I pull one slick lip into my mouth, lavishing it.

"Dear God," she gasps, twisting her hips to get away. "It's too much . . . I can't . . ."

"You want me to stop?" I ask, nibbling on the other lip.

"No, no, n-no," she chants, linking her legs at my back. I feel the disproportionate weight of the prosthetic leg heavier than the other, and thinking of her navigating the world, turning what should have been a disadvantage into an advantage, into a way of life and inspiration, not just for her but for hundreds of thousands of others, makes me want to treasure her even more. I start licking in earnest greed, getting sloppy with it. I lift under her thighs to spread her wider, bring her closer. I pinch her clit and kiss the valley between her legs until high, loud moans leak from her mouth and wetness spills from her body, dousing me with her passion.

I'm drowning in her complete satisfaction.

Chapter 12

Quinn

That feels so good.

Standing behind me, Ean plants his hands at my hips, bending to brush his lips along my nape. He opens his mouth over the sensitive skin there and sucks.

My hands shake and I can't get the key card from my purse. I give up and slump back on his broad chest, my head lolling against him. "If you keep that up, we'll never get inside."

"At this point, I'm not above doing it right here," he chuckles, his breath breezing through the short hair curing around my ears. "But let me try."

He takes the key and lets us in. As soon as we step inside, the air thickens with anticipation. With desire.

With uncertainty.

The moment of truth. Time to bare it all.

It's not that I'm self-conscious about my residual limb. I'm just unsure of how my *partner* will feel the first time. It's an important distinction. There have been times when guys thought they would be fine, but the reality of seeing me, not walking around on a flesh-colored prosthetic looking relatively "normal" and wearing Louboutins, but seeing an empty space where a limb should be,

159

disconcerted them. A rounded stump with a scar that looks like a happy face. It's not that I didn't know them, but sometimes they didn't know *themselves*. They assumed they'd be fine with it, but struggled to adjust. Those guys got shown the door. I don't need to be made to feel like a charity case, or like someone they had to work themselves up to fuck.

Ted and I never made it as far as having sex, so I never had to watch him school his features to hide distaste or discomfort, but I'm sure if we had, that's what I would have seen. I saw, too late, that he was that kind of guy.

I walk deeper into the lavishness of the Ritz's presidential suite. The sleek modernity, all stark lines and metal, could feel cold, but dark wood accents and Southern hospitality warm the space.

"We still okay?" Ean asks from the door.

"Yeah." I nod and smile at him over my shoulder. He smiles back, walks up to me, and runs his hands down my arms, linking our fingers. When he kisses me, he explores my mouth deeply, so deeply I taste my pussy on his tongue. The kiss grows hotter, rougher, until my lips sting and it makes me wet all over again. My panties are in his pocket, so the wetness trickles down my thighs. Our breathing comes heavy between our mouths, and he reaches down to squeeze my ass, one cheek in each hand.

"I want to fuck you," he whispers, resting his forehead against mine. "So very badly, Quinn, but if you aren't comfortable, if you don't want to anymore—"

"I do." I caress his full lips with my thumb, pushing into his mouth. He sucks down right away, pulling my thumb deeper into the cavern of his mouth, and every time he sucks, there's a corresponding twitch in my core. His passion is a pulley, and I respond to his slightest touch.

"Would you mind if I take a quick shower first?" I ask. "I don't want to break the mood, but I—"

"You already explained, and I'm fine. Take your time."

I nod and walk quickly to the bedroom and close the door, hearing Sports Center start on the other side right away. I grin and shake my head. He can't stay away from it for any amount of time.

I never know what I'll get in a hotel bathroom, though Willa's great about calling ahead to ensure the hotel accommodates my needs. It's nothing like my shower at home, of course, which I've outfitted with a bench, several grab bars, an adjustable hand-held showerhead and a pressure mixing valve so I don't burn myself with too-hot water. This is great, though. The walk-in shower has a bench. I start the water, then sit on the edge of the tub to remove my prosthetic. I peel the tight liner away from my stump and grab the antibacterial cleanser I use for the liner and my residual limb every day, and do a cursory cleanse. Even though I'm about to shower, I pump some of the cleanser into my hands and rub it on my stump while I'm here and it's easy.

With that done, I swing my legs over the side of the tub, set my liner on its drying rack and hop over to the shower where the collapsible walker I travel with is already set up. Showering can be perilous. Hopping around on wet tiles on one leg is a recipe for disaster, so the walker keeps me safe.

It's only been a few minutes since I left Ean, but thanks to the bench, I get through showering and washing my hair quickly and without incident. I pull myself up by the grab bar and use the walker to journey back to the side of the tub where I sit and dry off.

I didn't anticipate this happening, so I didn't pack any of my sexiest lingerie, but I do have a petrol blue short satin slip. A silvery frastaglio frames the plunging neckline and shows off my neck and breasts. I work hard to keep my body fit, healthy. I'm proud of it, but the inevitable nervousness of a partner seeing me without the prosthetic for the first time still lines the inside of my belly.

Taking a deep breath, I hop the few feet back toward the dining room, but stop to stand in the frame of the bedroom door. Ean's on the couch, muscled legs stretching out forever in front of him. His hands link behind his head as he watches television, a position which flexes the bulge of muscle in his arms. There's the slightest bit of nervousness, but it doesn't diminish the overwhelming roar of my body's need.

I want him.

And everything I've seen from him signals that he wants me—just as I am.

I clear my throat, and his head whips around toward the bedroom entrance. His mouth drops open slightly, and he grabs the remote to turn off the television. His eyes start at the top of my hair, wet and curling just the slightest bit, over my face, free of make-up. His gaze heats as it moves over my breasts, and my nipples tighten beneath the silk. The intensity of his stare feels like a touch. His eyes drift down farther, and I know what he sees. My slip hits mid-thigh, so for the first time he sees my stump floating in the air beside the lean, muscled curvature of my other leg. He drags his eyes back up to meet mine, and I'm relieved to see the desire hasn't cooled. If anything, his stare grows hotter the longer we are apart.

He stands and strides over to the door. He towers a foot over me, and I tip my head back to meet the dark eyes glowing with feeling that answers mine. Feeling not made of just desire and passion, but of need that goes beyond the quick fuck I pushed for the last time. A need for closeness and understanding. *Intimacy.*

"You look so beautiful," he breathes, his voice husky. "I don't even know where to start."

He dips his head, drives his hand into damp hair and fits his lips to mine. It's urgent and immediate, the push of his tongue inside my mouth. His body confesses his hunger in so many ways. The tightening of his fingers in my hair. The hoarse sounds in the back of his throat. The compulsive ravishment of his mouth, taking and taking and taking, a helpless hunger that his hard frame trembles with against me.

His hands slide to my ass, and he folds his arms under my butt, lifting me and walking with quick strides to the bed. Not lifting me like he's helping me, concerned that I can't walk, but lifting me *possessively*, like I'm his to carry, to lay down on the feathery bedding and claim. He stands over me, running his eyes all over my body, biting his lower lip and closing his eyes tightly.

"I'm going to try hard to be gentle" he says, his voice raw. "But I want you so much."

"I don't need gentle." I reach up to capture his hand with mine. "I need to be fucked."

My words set him off, and he wrenches the polo shirt over his head, rumpling the coarse wave of his short hair. With haste, he strips off his slacks and briefs and socks until he's naked at the end of the bed.

Good. God.

Ean's body is a map of discipline and hard work and muscle and sinew. His pectorals are full and swelling, tipped with dark nipples. Four stacks of abdominal muscles form a ridged ladder down his stomach, tapering to a narrow waist. He's a stallion, his thighs long, lean, and flexing. His calves are carved and shaped like teak wood.

And his dick.

In some atavistic response of mate recognizing mate, my legs spread as soon I see his cock hanging long and proud, framed by two huge balls that will fill my mouth completely. I swallow, remembering how I've wanted to blow him from the beginning.

"May I suck your dick?" I ask, breathless and thirsty.

His eyes flare and the strong column of his throat contracts with a deep swallow. Wordlessly, he climbs on the bed, spreading his thighs over my torso and shifting up until his cock hovers over my lips, just out of reach. I almost whimper with the need to taste him, to feel him scraping the walls of my throat. He makes no move to close the distance, waiting to see how bad I want it.

I want it bad.

I lift my head until his crown brushes my lips. His salty pre-cum slips into the corner of my mouth, and I flick my tongue to capture it.

"Shit," I gasp, pulling my tongue in, pressing it to the roof of my mouth so I can savor him fully. "You taste good, Jag."

Heavy breaths heave his chest and the muscles in his stomach. He spreads his thighs, one on either side of my head, a little wider, lowering himself by careful inches into my mouth.

"Mmmmm," I moan around the length of him slipping past my lips and to the back of my throat. I slide my mouth up and down, up and down, relishing the slick, hot hardness. I pull my head back, releasing his dick, angling to suck one of his balls.

"Fuck, Quinn," he roars. I lavish each ball until they glisten and the veins along his cock strain. He reaches down, grabs my chin, and pushes himself back into my mouth, and his hips piston with relentless thrusts, knocking him to the back of my throat.

"Are you okay?" He glances down at me. I nod almost frantically, afraid he'll stop before spilling down my throat. I want it. I want his very essence coating my mouth, rolling like a river into the deepest parts of me.

His movements are aggressive, and the gagging sounds I make, the tears pouring over my face, seem to spur him on. Gentle fingers mop at the wetness on my cheeks, and he slowly pulls out.

"Jag, no." I move my head to recapture his cock, but he presses his thumb to my lips. He shifts back and off the bed, running his eyes along my body sheathed in costly satin and silk.

"Let me show you," he says, his eyes tracking over me, his hands following, nudging the hem of my slip up, exposing my legs.

I'm still covered. He can't even see my pussy, but this is the most naked I've felt all night. I watch his face closely. I know the signs when a guy changes his mind—realizes this, *I'm* not for him. The shrinking cock. The awkward half-smile. The shifting eyes. The hesitant hands.

With Ean, there's none of that.

His mouth falls into a sober line, lending weight to this moment. He caresses my thighs, both my thighs, with steady, kneading hands. And his eyes, when they lift to meet mine, they burn hot with passion and tenderness and something else. Something I can't name.

"Thank you," he whispers.

Gratitude.

I couldn't name that look because I've never seen it in a man's eyes before we made love. Grateful that I'm sharing my body with him, sharing my secrets. Trusting him with my vulnerable truths and inevitable realities. He pushes the slip up a few more inches, glancing between my legs and swallowing deeply.

"In the car," he says. "I could taste you, smell you, but it was dark and I couldn't really see you. You are so fucking gorgeous, Quinn."

He slides his hands down, touching my knee and my stump with the same reverence, the same gentleness, and then he touches the aching valley between my legs. His fingers slipping, sliding through my wetness and my panting breaths are the only sounds in the room. His breathing grows harsh, his eyes fixed between my legs. He thrusts four fingers inside me.

"Ahhh." My back bows off the bed and my legs lift, widen, as I spread myself for him to go deeper. His fingers leave me only long enough to spread the juices up and down my pussy and asshole, and then all four fingers are back, aggressive. He withdraws, and slaps my clit.

"Jag." His name is ejected from my mouth and my hands dig into the sheets.

His fingers barrel back inside me, twisting, and I feel him in both holes, four fingers in my pussy, his thumb in my ass. With his other hand, he shoves the slip all the way up, bathing my stomach and breasts in cool air. He squeezes and twists one nipple, squeezes my breast so hard I cry out with pleasure on a knife's edge. I pump my hips, chasing my orgasm, chasing him, his touch, his fingers.

Invade. Retreat. Invade. Retreat.

The torturous rhythm makes war on my senses, battering my defenses until I'm howling. I'm weeping. I'm growling, reduced to a mass of helpless whimpers, clawing fingers, and a throbbing clit. I'm a staggering pulse, racing and under his command.

"Jag, I can't . . ." I hiccup, tears coursing down my face. "You have to fuck me."

"Not yet." He twists his fingers deeper in, his thumb deeper in. Pulls out, spreads the juices. Slaps my clit with the back of his hand.

And then I come.

So suddenly, so abruptly, my breath stalls. It's the shock of launching off a building, the free fall with no landing. The force of gravity presses into my chest. Pleasure uncoils from the base of my spine and spreads across my back, over my shoulders like oil. I dissolve, my bones and blood melting into the mattress, leaving me soaking in this glorious lethargy.

He rains kisses over my breasts, down my stomach, between my legs where he stops to lick, groaning as he takes my juices on his tongue. And then he kisses my legs, saving special, gentle kisses for my left one.

"Now," he whispers, tugging at the slip until it's over my head and gone. "Now we fuck."

A broken chuckle stumbles past my lips, and I watch his big body with dazed eyes. I absorb his affection with an overflowing heart. He is the most magnificent thing I've ever seen. A monument of a man, but not stone. He's muscle, flesh, and bone. He's goodness, tenderness, and kindness.

"How do you like it?" he asks softly. "Are there positions that are better? Or—"

"Let's just start with you on top," I reply with a lazy smile.

Missionary is easiest from a leverage perspective, but I also want to feel the weight of him pressing into me.

He reaches down to his pants on the floor and pulls a condom out, then slips it on with quick efficiency. He crawls onto the bed, hovering over me. Bracing himself with one hand on the bed, he pushes my hair back with the other, his fingers straying over my cheekbones and across my lips.

"Hi," he says with a smile.

"Hi," I whisper back, my grin growing.

He reaches down to stroke between my legs and then to position himself. Our eyes lock and he pushes in.

"Ah." I gasp because he's so big and it's been more than a year. My pussy clamps around him like I'm afraid he'll get away. Our bodies are joined at this tight and wet and hot point of contact.

"Shit," he groans, squeezing his eyes closed. "This is . . . you are . . . *Quinn.*"

He moves deeper, impossibly deeper, until I'm sure I can't take even another centimeter of him. Just when I think I'll combust, he pulls back and then thrusts in, over and over, fast, aggressive, unrelenting. I shift my hips, and he hits that secret spot that unlocks another room inside me, an inner court no one has entered. I'm falling, burning, crashing into a void of dark bliss. And with a roar and a muttered "Thank you. God, Quinn, thank you," into the curve of my neck, so does he.

Chapter 13

Ean

"**G**et back on defense!"

I love seeing a dunk as much as the next basketball fan, but sometimes I think it's made players want to show off more and pay less attention to the fundamentals of the game.

Take Clyde, a first-round draft pick coming to the Waves this upcoming season. When he goes up, his head is above the rim, but when he hits that floor, his fundamentals suck.

"We got a lot of work to do before the season starts," I tell him once we're done. "Back here tomorrow. Same time."

"Thanks, Coach," he says. "I know I got a long way to go."

"That you do." I nod to Jeremy and Reggie sitting on the bench, observing. I worked them over during the first thirty minutes. "Same goes for you. Back here tomorrow."

"Oh, I got a thing tomorrow," Reggie says with a grin. "Party at the *Playboy* mansion."

I stride over to him and lean into his face. "Don't be here tomorrow, and I will come to the *Playboy* mansion my damn self and drag your ass out of there like your mama when the streetlights come on. Am I clear?"

His eyes widen. "I'm a grown man, Coach."

"Yeah, a grown man taking up space on my roster and making more money than he's worth right now. How many invitations you think you'll get when the front office sends you down to the D-league?"

He gulps and nods. "Two o'clock?"

"Perfect."

We're packing up when Jeremy pulls out an ESPN magazine. It's the body issue. He whistles low, his eyes wide on the page.

"This chick is fine as hell."

"Yeah," Clyde agrees. "I don't care if she ain't got but one leg."

My head snaps up and I walk over to snatch the magazine from them. And there she is. Quinn, lowered into a runner's crouch, like she's poised to explode into motion. With her hands pressed to the ground, her extended arms hide the full, pert breasts I've tasted for myself. She's all long lines and sleek muscle, her ass, round and firm. Her ginger hair is mussed and her delicate profile belied by the determined set of her jaw. One sleek leg is stretched, and the prosthetic, one of her designs, is shiny carbon with flowers and vines lightly sketched on the surface. A thing of function and beauty.

"Ahem."

The clearing throat at the edge of the court grabs the attention of all four of us. I break out into a wide grin, but the other three gape, mouths hanging open. Their eyes dart from the beautiful woman on the page to the in-flesh version of her standing in front of them.

"Uh, sorry to interrupt," Quinn says, an uncertain smile and frown on her face. "I hope it's okay I just dropped in. You said you'd be here, and I was in town so . . ."

We stare at each other, ignoring the guys from my team.

"Oh." I turn to the astonished trio. "Quinn, this is Reggie, Jeremy and Clyde. They're rookies."

"Hi, rookies," she says, laughing and stepping forward with an outstretched hand.

They all shake hands. She stands in the midst of us towering over her like a little fairy among trees while we chat about the first year in the league and the upcoming awards season.

"Well, we better get going," Clyde says. "It was nice meeting you, Ms. Barrow."

"Yeah, nice meeting you," Billy says. "See you at the ESPYs."

They drift off, and once they're gone, I fold my arms under her ass and lift her up until our faces are level. The kiss is hot and wild and desperate. Her arms creep around my neck and her fingers twist in my hair. She wraps her legs around my waist and pulls back enough to see my face.

"Hi," she whispers, leaning forward for one last quick peck.

"Hi," I answer, catching her mouth and kissing her deeply again. "I missed you this week."

"I missed you, too. I was half-hoping you'd pop up at my event here in San Diego," she says with a teasing smile.

I grimace. "If the owners hadn't scheduled a meeting today at the same time, believe me, I would have been."

"It's all good," she says, stroking my neck. "It's about time I came to you."

"Got that right." I laugh.

She slides down my body until she lands on the court. "What were your guys snickering over like middle-schoolers when I came in?"

"That's a perfect description." I push back the fringe of hair falling into her eyes. "It was actually a photo of you in *ESPN* magazine. The body issue."

Her eyes go round. "Oh, my gosh. And I walked in while they were looking at that? Glad I didn't know."

"So you're home for a week?" I ask, bending to trail kisses down her neck. "I cannot keep my hands off you."

"You will not hear me complaining." She giggles. "And, yes. I'm home for a week before I go back out on the road." Her smile fades and she shuffles her feet a little. "I, um, was thinking about going up to Malibu for a few days. I have a place up there."

"Oh?" I brush a thumb over her cheekbone and lift her chin so our eyes meet. "Want some company?"

Her smile is a rising sun, glorious and blinding. "I was going to ask. Are you sure you can get away? I know the season—"

"Hasn't started yet. Once it does, it'll be hard for me to do much else, so we should take advantage of my free time now."

"We're both so in demand."

"Yeah, but I'm in." I dip to kiss the corner of her mouth. "Relationships take work, and work is something we're both really good at."

She shakes her head, a small smile sketched on her lips. "Are we in a relationship?"

My smile drops. "We better be. I hope we are. I told my mom we were getting married."

Her mouth drops open, but before she can express the panic in her eyes, she realizes I'm fucking with her. She punches me in the chest, her laugh echoing through the gym.

"You sneaky bastard. I should have known you were joking. Everybody thinks 'The Machine' is all stoic. I know what a cut-up you are."

"That's because you get to see what no one else does."

She tips up on her toes, wraps her arms around my neck again, and whispers in my ear. "Your huge cock?"

"That, too." I chuckle. "I show you everything." I sober, and look down at her in all seriousness. "I trust you with everything."

"I feel the same," she says, and she lifts her lashes to look at me. "Are we crazy? Saying these things, feeling these things so quickly?"

"I don't think so," I tell her softly. "You're right. It feels fast, but it feels right."

Epilogue

Quinn – Two Years Later

"Who are you wearing, Quinn?"

The question, yelled from the line of reporters and flashing cameras on the red carpet, makes me smile.

"Lotus Ross." I pull back the flap of the silky wrap dress to display the length of my Bionic Beauty leg, also shiny and sequined to match my dress.

"Does Lotus' GloUp brand have a maternity line in the works?" another asks.

I rub my huge belly and grin. "Maybe soon. Lo designed this one just for me."

"Enough questions," Ean barks, his perma-scowl firmly in place. "We need to get inside."

I wave as he half-drags, half-carries me down the rest of the red carpet.

"Jag, you're being ridiculous."

"No, I'm being considerate, understanding that just *maybe* a woman eight months pregnant might not want to stand around in the hot sun answering a series of inane questions about her dress."

He's not wrong. A small fire burns low in my spine. *This baby.*

"Are the ESPYs giving out an award for Husband of the Year tonight?"

"No." He opens the door for us to enter the building. "But I hear this cute redhead is getting the Jimmy V Perseverance Award."

"It's the only reason I'm here," I tell him with a smile and a quick press of my lower back.

His perma-scowl comes back with a vengeance. "I knew it."

He reaches around and digs knowing fingers into the muscles of my back. I slump forward and rest my head on his chest.

"That feels so good, baby. Keep doing that." I laugh and look up at him through my lashes. "Remember the first day we met, when you groped my back?"

His boom of laughter draws the eyes of a few people standing nearby. I'm not sure if it's because he's so loud, or because The Machine was heard actually laughing, a phenomenon I'm privileged to witness daily.

"That wasn't groping." His hands slide down from my back to cup and squeeze my ass. "*This* is groping."

"Ean," I squeak, looking around to see if anyone's noticing. "If there's a picture of me looking like the Good Year balloon and you groping my ass online tomorrow—"

"You'll what?" He bends to whisper in my ear. "Not give me a blow job? That's a lie. We both know how much you love my cock in your mouth."

My pussy amens that, clenching and flooding my panties at his dirty words in such a public place. My nipples go hard. He loves my third-trimester horniness, and provokes it every chance he gets. He knows I'm insatiable.

"If you don't want to find yourself getting screwed in a broom closet somewhere," I mutter, reaching between us to inconspicuously squeeze his dick, "you'll keep comments like that to a minimum."

"That's exactly what I want," he says, his voice low and husky. "To say I fucked America's Titanium Sweetheart in a broom closet."

"Soon as we get home, I want you naked and ready to service

your very pregnant wife," I tell him with a naughty smile. "Expect to put some time in *down there*."

"My mouth is watering just thinking about it." He tightens his grip on my ass.

"Welp, these panties are done."

"Good. Slip them off so I can put them in my pocket."

"Ean, you are supposed to be the reasonable, conservative, staid one in this marriage."

"I think we tossed that out the window in the parking lot of the Slutty Vegan."

I tip my head back and laugh, warmth filling my chest at the memory. "We haven't been back since."

"I'm scared we'll run into that poor traumatized driver who probably heard you screaming and moaning in the back seat."

Ean chased me down then—he wanted this thing that was only a possibility badly enough to run after it. To run after me.

"That was a great night," I say, blinking back sudden tears.

"Hey." He touches my cheek, frowning when his fingers come away wet. "Are you sure you're okay? Does your leg hurt? Are you wearing the thinner liner? The prosthetist said you should—"

"Jag, I'm okay." I reach up to caress the rigid line of his jaw. "Don't worry about me."

"It's my job to worry about you." He palms my big belly and frowns, his full lips tightening.

Apparently I don't do anything typical. Just shy of forty, I'm managing the slight risks getting pregnant when I'm older entails, but also the adjustments to my prosthesis. Because of weight gain there's a larger amount of soft tissue in my residual limb. Tissue breakdown and swelling can lead to alignment issues, which increases the chance of falls. All information I would prefer Ean had not been present for. I think that's when the perma-scowl made its first appearance.

"Maybe you could just stay back here and not sit out there," Ean says, watching me closely. "How are your hips? Those seats aren't the most comfortable."

"My hips are fine. I promise."

He bends and takes my bottom lip into his mouth, sucking hard, and steadily kneading the aching muscles in my lower back.

"I wish you hadn't worn those heels," he mutters into our kiss. "If I see you teeter once, I'm carrying you on that stage to accept the award."

I'm more concerned that if we don't sit down soon, he'll find a way for me not to accept the award at all, and will whisk me back home.

"This shoe is just a little tight," I say, faking a grimace. "Could we sit now?"

"Of course, baby." He guides me toward the theater entrance and we find our seats.

Once the ceremony begins, I release a long sigh of relief. I'm sitting. My feet are not aching. My back isn't hurting. My husband is not scowling. All's well with the world. I reach for Ean's hand.

"I love you," I whisper. "Coach of the Year."

He was his typical modest, self-effacing self when he won the distinction from the NBA a few weeks ago. "You're lucky I don't make you address me that way all the time."

"I'll try it tonight. Let's see how it sounds with your big dick in my mouth."

"Dammit, Quinn," he grits, shifting in his seat.

"Shhh!" I mock-frown. "Everything's not about you, Jag. It's time for my award."

He rolls his eyes good-naturedly and I grab his hand, bringing it to my lips for a quick kiss.

When they run the video package that accompanies my award, I'm unexpectedly emotional. Pregnancy hormones probably, but it's also seeing that young girl at the Olympic trials. Someone took the photo minutes before I ran my last race. I looked right into the camera and waved, having no idea how my life was about to change. Seeing the pictures after the fall—the sad girl with the hollow eyes and the bandages at her wrist, a testament of her despondence. I want to grab her face and tell her to hang in there. That there's an amazing life waiting for her if she can just get out of that bed and chase it. And then I watch the miraculous evolution from that shell of a person into the woman I am today.

When my name is called, Ean stands and walks me, not only to the stage, but up the stairs. He cocks one brow when I try to tell him it's not necessary. His look reminds me if it were left to him, he'd be carrying me onstage, so I relent. He doesn't return to his seat, but slips off into the wings so he can help me when I'm done. I wait for the applause to die and for everyone standing to sit.

"Wow." I lift the statue and shake my head. "This is something else. I'm overwhelmed."

I force myself to look out at the audience even though I feel tears stinging my eyes. *Damn hormones!*

"If you had told me all those years ago that I'd be receiving an award for perseverance, I would have laughed in your face."

I spread a wry smile around the large theater. "Actually, I probably would have cried in your face. I hadn't found my fight then, and you have to. If you're facing something that seems insurmountable, some circumstance that feels like it will break you, listen to me."

I give them the stern look I use on myself in the mirror when self-pity tries to show its ass. "If you're still alive, there's still hope. There are not enough pieces life can shatter you into to not be whole again. Maybe not the same, but whole in the ways that count."

I gesture to the large screen behind me. "I will never be that fresh-faced girl who believed life owed me something. Life doesn't owe you shit. Good things, bad things, they happen to us all, and most of the time, we have no control over any of it. It's not how life tries to break you that's the story. Life tries to break *everyone*. The story isn't that you fell. The story is that you got up again and again and again. I got up."

I don't even care that tears are streaming down my face now. "I got up and learned to walk again. It's not the smooth stride it was before. There will always be a hitch in my step. My body's not flawless. I have seven surgeries worth of scars that made sure of that. My body may not be flawless, but it's strong."

I swipe at my tears and manage to laugh. "They call me America's Titanium Sweetheart and the Bionic Beauty. People assume what's titanium, what's bionic, is my leg. Wrong. My *will* is titanium. My *spirit* is bionic. *I* am made of steel, and hard times don't break me."

I pause, sniff, and sweep the crowd with another firm look. "Hard times make me. I was built by adversity and setbacks and shitty circumstances. I won't cry anymore for what I lost because I've gained too much. A career I never even imagined. Friends who see me beyond the things I can't do for all the things I can."

I search the crowd until I find Banner sitting beside her husband Jared, her face tear-streaked like mine.

"Banner." My voice breaks, and I bow my head, emotion stealing my voice for a moment. "Thank you, girl. When everyone thought it was over, you convinced me I was just getting started. You're that rare person who sees the good and dreams the best even when things are darkest. We can't do anything to deserve friends as good as you. We're either blessed with them or we aren't, and I'm so glad I have you."

She covers her mouth and nods. Years of hard work and faith and the unconditional love of best friends unite us even across the large room.

I turn my head and find Ean standing in the wings, his face wet when I've never seen him cry. "I'm grateful for a husband who chased me, loved me, never gave up on me." I bite my lip to keep more tears from falling. "I wasn't sure men like you even existed. You have loved me so perfectly. What we have is a miracle, and I want to spend the rest of my life doing impossible things with you, Jag."

I turn back to the crowd and hold the statue in the air. "Thank you for tonight and for all the support."

I walk off, ignoring the standing ovation. I have eyes only for my big, beautiful husband. I make straight for his arms, and he holds me tight, sniffing against my ear and stroking my hair. We cling to each other for long minutes. I shake against him, sobbing with no sorrow. With a joy so pure and deep I couldn't describe it to someone with words. For some feelings words don't exist. This closeness, this love is a language all on its own.

"I'm so proud of you, Quinn," he finally says, his voice still husky. "You're the best thing that's ever happened to me, and I'm so glad our daughter will have you as an example."

I can't wait to tell her what beauty really is. That it's not the shiny things, but the gritty things that make true beauty. The character formed when things are hard. The kindness when you could be cruel. It's empathy when you could settle for not understanding. It's seeing those others deem invisible. It's all the things I hope I've shown the world.

But more importantly, it's all the things I learned to show myself.

***

Want to start at the beginning?
Read on for an excerpt from Long Shot,
book 1 of the HOOPS Series.
Please note that Long Shot has graphic depictions of intimate partner
violence not involving the hero. That content is not in the following
excerpt, but throughout the full novel.

Long Shot Excerpt

Tomorrow is my father's birthday.

Or it would have been. He died fifteen years ago when I was six, but in the biggest moments, the ones that count the most, it feels like he's with me. And on the eve of the biggest night of my life, I hope he can see me. I hope he's proud.

Tomorrow's the most monumental game of my life. By all rights, my ass should be safely tucked away in my hotel room, not out killing time at some dive. I toss back a handful of bar nuts and sip my ginger ale. At the table next to me, they just ordered another round of beers. God, what I wouldn't give for something strong enough to unwind these pre-game jitters, but I never drink before a game. And tomorrow isn't just any game.

I glance at my watch. Fifteen minutes late? That's not Coach Kirby. He's the promptest man I know. His name flashes across my screen just as I'm considering calling him. I push away the bowl of nuts and the niggling feeling that something must be wrong.

"Hey, Coach."

"West, hey." His voice carries a forced calm that only confirms something's off. "I know I'm late. Sorry."

"No, it's cool. Everything okay?"

"It's Delores." His voice cracks over his wife's name. Basketball is my high school coach's second love. From the day I met him my freshman year at St. Joseph's Prep, I knew Delores was his first.

"She okay?"

"She . . . well, we were at the hotel, and she started having chest pains and trouble breathing." Coach's worried sigh comes from the other end. "We're here at the emergency room. They're running all these damn tests, and—"

"Which hospital?" I'm already on my feet, digging out my wallet to pay the modest bill. "I'm on my way."

"The hell you are." The steel that worked all the laziness out of me for four years stiffens his tone. "You're playing tomorrow night in the National Championship. The last place you need to be is in some hospital waiting room."

"But, Delores—"

"Is my responsibility, and I'm handling it."

"But, I can—"

"Your folks get into town yet?" He steamrolls over my protest to close the subject.

"No, sir." I pause, checking my exasperation. "Matt had to work today. He and my mom are flying in tomorrow."

"And your stepbrother?"

"He's stuck in Germany. Some event for one of his clients." My stepbrother and I may not share blood, but we share a love of sports. Me, on the court. Him, off, as an agent.

"Sorry he won't be there," Coach says. "I know how close you two are."

"It's alright." I play off my disappointment. "I've got my mom and Matt. And you, of course."

"Sorry I can't make it to the bar, though why your ass wanted to go out the night before the big dance in the first place is beyond me."

"I know, Coach. I just needed . . ." What *do* I need? I know the playbook inside and out and have watched so much film my eyes started crossing.

I'm restless tonight. Years of sacrifice, mine and my family's, have gotten me here. And I couldn't have done it without the man on the other end of the line. Coach has invested a lot in me over the last eight years, even after I graduated high school and moved on to college. When scouts and analysts urged me to go pro a year early, he convinced me to stay and finish my degree. To shore up my fundamentals and mature before going to the draft. But the man who passed his DNA on to me—his wingspan, his big hands, his long, lean body, and I guess even his love for the game—is the one I keep thinking about tonight.

My father.

I wasn't sure who this moment should be shared with, but I knew it wasn't my teammates trolling for girls in some rowdy bar. Even though they can only get so rowdy the night before a game, that didn't appeal to me.

"Whatever you need, get it, and get out of there," Coach says, snapping me back into the moment. "Get your ass back to the hotel. Mannard *will* bench you for breaking curfew, even before the National Championship. Don't get too big for your breeches."

"Yes, sir. I know."

Between Coach's take-no-shit leadership and my stepfather's military background, the sirs and ma'ams come naturally. Discipline and respect were non-negotiable in both their regimes.

"I need to go," Coach says. "Doctor's coming."

"Keep me posted."

"I will." He pauses for a moment before continuing. "You know I'll be at the game tomorrow if there's any way it's humanly possible. I just need to make sure Delores is okay. She's the only reason I would miss it. I'm proud of you, West."

"I know. Thanks, Coach." Emotion scorches my throat, and I struggle to hold my shit together. My dad's birthday, the pressure of tomorrow's game, and now Delores in the hospital—I'm staggering under the cumulative weight of this day, of all these things, but I make sure none of it makes it into my voice when I speak again. Coach's got enough to worry about without thinking I'm not ready for tomorrow. "Do whatever you need to. Delores comes first."

"I hope to see you tomorrow," he continues gruffly. "You shoot the damn lights out of that place."

"Yes, sir. I plan to. Call me when you know something."

I don't even bother finding the server or asking for the check. Instead, I leave a twenty on the table, more than enough to cover my tepid ginger ale. I have another few hours to kill before curfew, but if Coach isn't coming to ease my nerves, then I may as well head back to the hotel. I'll try to slip in without running into my teammates.

I'm almost at the door when an outburst from the far end of the bar stops me.

"Bullshit!" a husky, feminine voice booms. "You know good and damn well that's a shit call."

Just shy of the threshold, I turn to see the woman who's cussing like a sailor. Curves punctuate her lean, tight body: the indentation of her waist in a fitted T-shirt, the rounded hips poured into her jeans. She jumps from her stool and leans forward, her body taut with outrage, her fists balled on the bar, and her eyes narrowed at the flat screen. She must be a good seven inches over five feet. A guy my height gets used to towering over everyone else, but I like a woman with a little height. Her hair, dark and dense as midnight, is an adventure, roaming wild and untamed around her face in every direction, drifting past her shoulders. She looks pissed, her wide, full mouth tight, and the sleek line of her jaw bunched.

The beautiful face paired with all that attitude has me intrigued. Even if I'm not getting laid tonight, I can at least get distracted from the pressure that's been crushing me all day. Hell, crushing me for the last few weeks, if I'm honest. I want to shake off the melancholy thoughts my father's death always wrap around me—thoughts of what we missed. What we lost. Seeing her all fired up and cussing at the television, swearing at the refs, lightens some of the load I've been carrying. I find myself walking straight toward the one thing that has penetrated the thick wall of tension surrounding me since we advanced to the NCAA championship a few days ago.

"Asshole," she mutters, settling her denim-clad ass back onto the barstool. "No way that was a flagrant foul."

I take the empty stool beside her, glancing up at the screen replaying the last sequence. "Actually, I'm pretty sure that *was* a flagrant foul." I grab a fistful of nuts from the bowl between us.

"You're either as blind and dumb as the ref," she says, eyes never leaving the screen, "or you're trying to pick me up. Either way, I'm not impressed."

My handful of nuts freezes halfway to my mouth. I have a shot at college player of the year, have been big man on campus for four years, and was on ESPN's *Plays of the Week* by tenth grade. No girl has shot me down since middle school, but I never shy away from a challenge.

"Just making conversation." I shrug and swing my knees around to face her. "Though if you want to be picked up, I might be able to accommodate."

She finally deigns to look at me. Her heart-shaped face is arresting, a contrast of fierce and delicate. She has high cheekbones and dark brows that slash over a button nose and hazel eyes. *Hazel* is too flat a word to describe all the shades of green and brown and gold. I've never seen eyes quite like these. Several colors at once. Several things at once. I wonder if the girl behind them is as multi-dimensional.

"I wouldn't want to wear you out before your big game tomorrow." The corners of her lips pinch like she's trying her best not to laugh at me.

That gives me pause. So she knows who I am. That would usually work in my favor, but I have a feeling she's not your run-of-the-mill ball groupie. "You're a fan?"

Unsurprisingly, one brow crooks, and she rolls her eyes before turning her attention back to the game. The bartender approaches, a bottle of liquor in hand.

"What'll ya have?" He sets the Grey Goose on the bar, toggling a speculative glance between me and the woman ignoring me.

"Could I get a ginger ale, please?"

He smirks, trading out the Goose for a ginger ale he pulls from the fridge under the bar. Filling a glass with the fizzy drink and setting it in front of me, he angles his head to peer under the brim pulled low over my brow.

"August West?" A grin lights his face.

I nod but put my finger to my lips, hoping to quiet him so I can flirt in peace. I don't feel like signing autographs and being pelted with well wishes. I'm not even in the NBA yet, but ever since our team made the Sweet Sixteen, the media has homed in on me for some reason, elevating my profile and making it harder to remain anonymous.

"I get it." The bartender nods knowingly, his voice dropping to a conspiratorial whisper. "Avoiding the crazy, huh?"

"Something like that." I look back to the super fangirl, whose attention remains riveted on the screen. "What's the lady having?"

"A beer she can pay for herself." She slides me a crooked smile and takes a sip of her half-full glass.

"Oooooh." The bartender's beer belly, an occupational hazard, shakes with a deep chuckle. He gives me a commiserating look before ambling down the length of the bar to his other customers.

"So, you come here often?" *I can't believe that just came out of my mouth.*

The face she makes says she can't believe it either.

"Next you'll ask what's a nice girl like me doing in a place like this." The humor in her eyes removes some of the sting.

"You think my game is that weak?"

She side-eyes me, extending both brows as high as they'll go. "We talking on the court or off?"

"Ouch." I wince and tilt my head to consider her. "And here I thought you'd be a sweet distraction until curfew."

"I'm not anyone's distraction," she says. "Especially not some player looking to let off testosterone."

"Assumptions and judgments." I shake my head in mock disappointment. "Didn't they tell you not to judge a book by its cover? You can't possibly know—"

"August West, six foot six, Piermont College starting point guard, deadly from behind the arc, off-the-charts basketball IQ, and Naismith finalist. Six-foot-ten-inch wingspan and forty-inch vertical." Her sharp eyes slice over me from the brim of my cap all the way down to the Nikes on my feet, before returning to the game onscreen.

"Your hops may be Jordan-esque, but your D could use some work." A laugh slips past her lips. "And that's not an assumption. I know that for a fact."

I have to laugh because Coach Mannard has been after me all season—for the last four years, actually—to improve on defense. My three-pointers make the highlight reel, but he's just as concerned with the fundamentals that will make me a better all-around player. Apparently, so is she.

"So they keep telling me." I turn my back to the bar, propping my elbows on its edge, and consider her with new respect. "How do you know so much about basketball?"

"You mean because I'm a girl and should be watching cheering matches?" Her glare is all indignation.

"Um . . . you mean tournaments? Even I know they're called cheer *tournaments*, not matches."

"Well look at that." She spreads a thick layer of sarcasm over the words. "You know girl stuff and I know boy stuff. Is it opposite day?"

She turns her attention back to the screen like she couldn't care less that she just impressed the hell out of me. Guys, we talk shit, and never more so than when it's about sports. A woman who can talk sports *and* talk trash? A fucking sparkling unicorn. She gives as good as she gets, this one. Hell, she may give *better* than she gets. There's a spark to her, a confidence I want to see more of.

A lot of girls just reflect. They figure out what you like so they can get in with a baller. This one has her own views, stands her own ground and doesn't give a damn if I like it.

I like it.

"Since you know so much about me," I say, "it's only fair I learn something about you."

She turns her head by slow centimeters, eyes still locked to the screen as if it's killing her to look away from the game. Her expression, those changeable eyes, warm and soften just a little. "What exactly would you like to know?"

"Your name would be a good start."

Her lips twist into a grin. "My family calls me Gumbo."

"Gumbo?" I almost choke on my ginger ale. "Because you have big ears?"

I risk touching her, pushing back a clump of wild curls. The whorl of her ear is downright fragile, and strands of dark hair cling to the curve of her neck.

"Not Dumbo." She laughs and pulls away so her hair slips through my fingers. "*Gumbo,* like the soup."

"I knew that." I really did, but I had to get inventive if I was going to steal a touch without drawing back a stump. "So why Gumbo?"

She hesitates, and for a moment it seems I wasn't breaking through like I thought. She finally gives a "what the hell" shrug and goes on.

"You may not hear the accent now, because it's been years since I lived there, but I'm originally from New Orleans."

Now that she says it, I do detect something reminiscent of that city in her voice. A drawn-out drawl spiced with music and mystery.

"My family moved to Atlanta after Katrina." She gives a puff of air disguised as a laugh. "But I'm NOLA, through and through. I come from good Creole stock. As if Creole wasn't already mixed up enough, my father's German and Irish."

I think the ambiguity of her beauty is part of her appeal. Something elusive and indefinable. I would never have guessed the ethnicities that coalesced to make a face like hers—the wide, full lips, copper skin and striking bone structure. I don't think I've ever seen anyone like her. Hers is not a face you would soon forget. Maybe never.

"I'm a mix of everything the bayou could come up with," she continues, taking a sip of her drink. "So my cousin says I had more ingredients than—"

"Gumbo," I finish with her. We share a smile, and she nods. "So you're a mutt like me."

"I wasn't gonna say anything." Her eyes run over my face and hair, my looks almost as ambiguous as hers. "But now that you mention it . . ."

"Lemme show you something." I pull out my phone, flipping through the photos until I land on a picture of my family from a camping trip a few years ago. "Here."

She takes the phone, her smile fading at the corners. I know what she sees. My mother smiles into the camera, her auburn hair a fiery halo around her pale face in the winter sun. My stepfather and stepbrother stand at her shoulder, both tall blondes.

And then there's me.

My hair cut close to tame the dark curls that can never decide which way to grow. My skin is the color of aged dark honey, and my eyes are gray as slate. I couldn't look less like a part of the family if I tried.

"One of these things is not like the others." I grin over the rim of my glass, sipping my ginger ale. "I guess I'm gumbo, too."

She returns my smile and my phone, but the humor slowly fades from her expression. Curiosity clouds her eyes when she looks back at me, but whatever that question is, she's not voicing it.

"What?" I finally ask.

"What do you mean *what*?"

"Just seemed like you wanted to say something."

For a second, her face shutters, and I think she won't tell me, but she glances up, a smile settling on her lips after a few seconds.

"Did you ever feel like you didn't quite fit anywhere?" Her words come so softly, competing with the revelry in the bar. I lean in to hear until our heads almost touch. "I mean, like you were always kind of in between?"

Her question echoes something I haven't articulated to many people but often felt. I sometimes felt displaced in my mother's new family. I may not look a lot like my African–American father, but I look nothing like anyone in the family I have left. Most kids were one thing or the other and clumped together based on that. It left me sometimes feeling adrift. Basketball—that rim, that rock—became the thing I clung to.

"I think I know what you mean." I clear my throat before going on. "My father died when I was really young, and my mom remarried not too long after. It took me a while to adjust to everything, especially being different when all I wanted was to fit in."

"I get that," she says.

I shrug and turn down the corners of my mouth.

"Thanks to basketball, I started worrying less about fitting in and more about standing out." I roll the glass between my palms. "But even then, yeah, I sometimes felt . . . I don't know. Displaced."

"Me, too. My skin was lighter than just about everyone's in my neighborhood. My hair was different." She shakes her head, the movement stirring the air around us with the scent of her shampoo, some mix of citrus and sweet. "Most girls there assumed I thought I was better than they were, when I would have given anything to look like everyone else. To fit in. I had my cousin Lo for a few years, but besides her, I kind of just had myself."

What was that like for her? A beautiful anomaly in the Ninth Ward. Maybe I don't have to wonder. Maybe I know firsthand.

"It got kinda lonely, huh?" I ask.

"Yeah, it did." She circles the rim of her glass with an index finger. Her lashes lower like that might hide her memories from me, hide her pain, but it's in her voice. I recognize it.

"Sometimes, even when we had a full house," I say, dropping my voice for just our ears, "I'd end up in the backyard shooting hoops by myself until it got dark."

Like there's some magnetic center, our bodies have turned in toward each other. Our confidences enshroud us, blocking out the ribald conversation, the impromptu karaoke across the room, the wild response to the games on the flat screens. It's just us two misfits. A few minutes with a complete stranger, and I suddenly feel understood in a way that's always been hard to find.

"You get used to being alone," she finally says.

"What about your mom? You guys close?"

"Close?" She squints one eye and tips her head back. "Not

really. She's made a lot of sacrifices for me, and it's never been easy. She's strong, a survivor, and I respect that, but I haven't always agreed with her choices. I can't remember my mother ever holding down a job for more than a few weeks."

"How'd you guys get by?"

"She's a beautiful woman." She raises cautious eyes, like she expects me to judge. "She used to say there's always some man willing to take care of a beautiful woman."

I don't know what to say to that. My mom is a beautiful woman, too, but I can't imagine her living that way—relying on just the physical—because she started teaching when my dad died and has worked hard ever since.

"You're a beautiful woman." I nudge her knee lightly with mine. "And I bet you can take care of yourself."

A smile starts in her eyes and eventually spreads to her lips. "Thank you."

I don't have to ask which compliment she's thanking me for.

"My aunt is older than my mom by two years," she continues. "It's what my mom saw her do. It's what they saw their mother do. They used what they had to get what they needed."

She sighs before sipping her drink and going on. "My aunt relocated with us to Atlanta after Katrina, and they might have changed zip codes, but they didn't change tactics. Apparently, men all over will take care of beautiful women."

"Besides your cousin, were you close to anyone else in your family?"

"Just Lotus." A frown shadows her expression. "She went to live with my great-grandmother south of the city and I stayed in New Orleans, but when she moved to Atlanta for college a few years ago, we got close again."

She shakes her head like she's dislodging thoughts, memories. "Enough about my family dysfunction. What about you? Perry West was your dad, right?"

"You know about my dad?" I ask.

"Yeah, sure." Sympathy fills her eyes when they meet mine over our drinks. "Losing him that way—it had to be tough."

"Yeah." I shrug, a casual rise and fall of my shoulders that doesn't hint at how tough it was. "He was a great player."

"He had an incredible long-range shot." She smiles ruefully. "How long was he in the league?"

"The car crash happened in the middle of his second season." I was young, but I still remember his funeral. His teammates were all there, tall as skyscrapers to my six-year-old eyes. "Tomorrow's his birthday."

"No way." Her eyes go wide. "You're playing in the freaking National Championship on your dad's birthday?"

I nod, allowing myself to smile for the first time over this monumental twist of fate. It's a long time since my mom was married to my dad, but she probably remembers that tomorrow's his birthday. We haven't talked about it, though. It feels like I'm the only one who knows it, and now this beautiful gumbo girl knows, too.

"Is tomorrow for him?" Her eyes never leave my face, her intent focus drawing me into her.

"It feels like it. You know? Like what are the odds? I keep wondering if he knows how far I've come. If he can see." I let out a soft laugh, watching her face for signs that she thinks I'm an idiot. "Does that sound stupid?"

"Not at all. I don't know what happens after we're gone, but I hope he can see. He'd be proud of you, no matter how the game goes tomorrow."

"I hope so." I lean in a little closer, giving her the same attention she afforded me. "What about your father? The German and Irish in your gumbo?"

She smiles, but it's a tight curve of her lips.

"He was German and Irish. That's about all I know." Her harsh laugh ripples through the pool of quiet we've made here in our corner of the bar. "Well, I also know he had a wife and kids. My mother was just . . . a side chick, I guess. He paid her rent while they were together, but right after I was born he moved on. So did she. He never came around asking about me. She never offered much explanation for his absence."

"And now? Nothing?"

"We left everything in the Ninth when we moved to Atlanta." Her shoulders lift and fall with a carelessness I don't buy. "He could still be in New Orleans. He may have died when the levees broke. Who knows? It's never made me much difference."

She flashes me another tight smile, signaling that she's done with the topic.

"How'd we get into all *that* stuff?" She points her finger at me in mock accusation. "*You*, sir, are a good listener. Sneaky way to distract a girl from the fact that her team's losing."

I glance up at the game, grabbing her segue out of deeper waters like a lifeline. "You a Lakers fan?"

"Die hard purple and gold." She folds her arms on the bar and leans forward, her eyes back on the screen. "New Orleans didn't have a team when I was growing up."

"Well they're getting crushed tonight," I offer unnecessarily, hoping to get a rise out of her. Of course, it works, and she goes on a diatribe defending the storied Lakers legacy, though it's taken such a beating lately.

Through halftime and the last two quarters, we squeeze in a lot of conversation between plays. She wants to work in sports marketing and has several internship opportunities that might pan out after graduation. It seems like most of her stories eventually circle back to her cousin Lotus, the ambitious badass fashion student who always has her back. For my part, I avoid rehashing all the things she already knows about me: the numbers on stat sheets and the stories that have been looping on all the sports shows. Instead, I tell her about my mom, about Coach, about the philosophy class that's kicking my ass. We cover everything from minutiae to monumental in the time it takes the Lakers to get blown out.

"What *did* get you so into basketball?" I ask her during a fourth-quarter commercial break.

"I dunno." She studies her beer, probably long gone flat. "One of my mom's guys, Telly, lived with us for a while when I was around ten." She leans one elbow on the bar, giving me a frank look. "He was one of the few good ones who stuck around for a little bit. He loved basketball. Loved the Lakers and we'd watch the games together." She chuckles, making track marks with her finger-tips in the condensation coating her glass. "On game nights, we'd order pineapple pepperoni pizza and drink root beer floats."

"What happened?" I sip on my third ginger ale. "To Telly, I mean?"

She answers first with a little shake of her head. "He outstayed his welcome, I guess." Her eyes drift to the screen, maybe an excuse to look away. Or maybe the game really has grabbed her attention. Lakers have the ball. "Someone else came along with more money. Mom traded up."

"You ever see him, talk to him again?"

Her eyes abandon the screen, and for a few quiet moments, she studies the bar top. "No."

The word comes low and husky. After a moment she looks back up, flashing me a half-teasing grin. "But I still like pizza and root beer when I watch the Lakers."

"No pizza on the menu here?" I mumble around a handful of nuts.

"Beggars can't be choosers." The smile she shares with me morphs into a scowl when the final score displays onscreen. "Another one for the 'L' column. Shit calls all night, ref."

"Really? Shit calls?" I glance from the game back to her face with skepticism. "Nothing to do with the fact that the team is aging and plagued by injuries the last few seasons? End of an era, if you ask me."

"Bite your tongue," she snaps, but there's a playful glint in her eyes. "You could end up going to the Lakers. Have you thought of that?"

"Who knows where I'll end up?" I slant my smile at her. "I'm hoping for the Stingers."

"Baltimore?" A frown crinkles her eyebrows before clearing. "Oh! Your hometown, huh?"

"I mean, it happened for LeBron in Cleveland. He played where he grew up, for the Cavs."

"True. Why do you want to stay close to home? You a mama's boy?"

My laugh booms over the TV commentators analyzing the Lakers' loss in the background. "My mom's pretty awesome, but that wouldn't keep me close to home." I stare into my ginger ale instead of at her, a little uncomfortable to express my reasons. "I just want to do something for the place that did so much for me. I was in the Boys and Girls Club. I had amazing teachers, especially in middle school when a lot of my friends started going off the rails. The community center's where I fell in love with basketball."

Self-consciousness burns my face, and I shrug. "My whole childhood was there, and that community made it a good one."

In the beat of silence after I finish, I glance up to find a slight smile on her face and warm eyes that meet mine easily.

"That's cool," she offers simply, and I'm glad she doesn't make it a big deal even though it must be obvious it's important to me. "So, you ready for the draft?"

I appreciate the shift of subject. It's not likely I'll go to Baltimore, and I don't let many people know how much it would mean to me. "I am, but it's all happening so fast." A dry chuckle rattles in my throat. "The NBA was some distant fantasy when I was in the eighth grade. Now it's right here, and unless something goes really wrong, it's actually happening. I just hope . . ."

My words trail off, but my uncertainty remains. It's not even about my ability to play at the next level. I know I'm prepared for that. It's all that comes with it that I'm not sure I'm ready for.

"You'll do great." Her slim fingers close over my hand, gripping the glass. "You'll be an amazing player."

Just that light pressure, just seeing her hand with mine, feels good. Something about the sight levels the unevenness I've felt all day and unlocks words I haven't said to anyone.

"I want to be more than just a player. I want to use my degree. I want a business. I want a family." It feels like a confession. "To be a good husband. A good father. This world I'm entering in a few months, I've seen it devour guys. We work toward this all our lives, and an injury, age, a bad trade, whatever—can end it overnight. If the game has eaten up your priorities, turned you into someone you never wanted to be, what's the point?" I laugh self-consciously. "I probably sound—"

"You sound too good to be true," she interrupts, her hand still resting on mine. "Guys in your position, the night before the big game, right on the edge of the draft—these aren't things most of them are thinking about."

She props her chin in the palm of her free hand, a slow smile working its way to her mouth. "You're special." She bites her lip, lifting her hand away from my fingers, dropping her eyes to the bar top scarred by a million glasses and a million moments before ours. "I'm glad I met you."

That sounds suspiciously like the beginning of goodbye. Like she's ready to close the door on this surreal chapter.

I can't let that happen. A night like this, a connection like this— it's singular. After tomorrow's game, my future will literally be a little ball bouncing around in the NBA Draft Lottery. I may end up playing for a team I don't like, living in a place I won't get to choose.

But tonight, I have control. I have choices, and I choose her. To get to know her. To woo her. To earn her trust. All I need is time.

But time seems to be the one thing we don't have.

"Closing." The bartender drags our empty glasses toward him and wipes down the surface in front of us. "You ain't gotta go home, but you gotta get out of here."

I hadn't noticed the bar emptying around us, but we're nearly the last ones left.

"Good luck tomorrow, West," the bartender says, sliding two checks across the freshly-wiped bar.

"Thanks." I stand and snatch both of them before she can even look at hers.

"Give me that." She lunges toward me, but I hold the check over my head, completely out of her reach.

She stumbles into me, her soft breasts pressing against my chest. I want to wrap my arms around the stretch of sensuous lines and curves that make up her body. With her check still suspended over my head, I slide my other hand down her back, investigating her shape beneath the clingy cotton. I palm the dip at her waist, drawing her a few inches closer until her warmth, her clean scent, surrounds me.

She blinks up at me, bright eyes darkening and widening, the green and gold lost in sable. Desire starbursts her irises. We've barely acknowledged the current humming between our bodies, the electricity running under the surface of our easy conversation, until just now. Until I lured her into me with a little slip of paper.

"Let me buy your drinks." I can't remember ever wanting a woman the way I want her. I don't just want to bury my hands in all that dark hair, or to discover for myself how sweet her lips taste, or to explore her body. I want more of her memories, her secrets—to accept an invitation she hasn't extended to anyone else.

Her lashes lower, shielding her eyes from mine, but she can't hide her body's response—the way all the places she's soft seem to seek out the places I'm hard and unyielding. How her breath stutters over her lips in little pants.

"Um, okay." She steps back until we're no longer touching, clearing some of the huskiness from her voice before going on. "Thanks. I could have . . . well, thanks."

Neither of us speaks on our way to the door. I find myself slowing to match her shorter stride. We watch each other from the corners of our eyes, the silence between us pulsing with possibility. Once outside, we're tucked away under an awning with the still-bustling city just beyond our patch of sidewalk. Inside, surrounded by people and noise and the action of the game, the conversation came so effortlessly. The confessions and admissions I'd never made to anyone else flowed right out of me. And now, it's just us and I'm not sure what to say to keep her here, but I know what I've been feeling, what we've been doing, can't end tonight.

There's this part in *Spanglish*, one of Adam Sandler's chick flicks. He and his kids' nanny share dinner at his restaurant. It's just one meal, a few hours. The narrator, the nanny's daughter, says, "My mother has often referred to that evening at the restaurant as the conversation of her life." I'm pretty sure I rolled my eyes when I heard it and said, 'That was *some* conversation.'

But now, with her, standing at the edge of goodbye, all I can think is . . . that was *some* conversation.

The streetlight and the moon illuminate things the dimness of the bar hid—the amber in her hair I thought was just black, the length of her lashes casting shadows on her cheeks while she studies the ground. We both seem to be searching for words. It's as if we've crammed so much into the last few hours that there are no words left—none left for me, anyway. All I have is feeling. *Need.* I need to touch her, to kiss her—I need something physical to reassure me this encounter really happened. That this isn't the end.

When you're a foot taller than a girl, it's hard to smoothly go in for a kiss, so I don't try for smooth. I'm careful, though. I lift her chin with one finger, persuading her eyes up to meet mine. I cup her cheek and lower my head until I'm hovering over those lips that look so soft I have to hold myself back from devouring them; I have to control my need to taste her right away. My body revs, demands. My heart slams into my rib cage. My dick is hard. Want sizzles through every cell of my body.

"August." She pulls her chin away and presses her hand to my chest, but not to explore. To gently push me back. I hold my breath, waiting to see what this means, this small space she's put between us.

Her head drops forward until the dark cloud of hair eclipses her face, hides her expression. "I'm sorry." She steps back, running a hand through her hair. "I-I can't."

I want to bring her close again. "It's okay. I get it, of course. We just met."

I link our fingers. Even that brief contact stirs my senses. I check the roar of my body, hoping my erection doesn't betray me.

"We can just talk. We can go to your place, if you're not far." I lift her chin so I can see her eyes. So she can see that I mean it. Despite the absolute inferno raging under my skin, it's enough. "We can do whatever you want."

As little, as much—let's just keep doing *something*. Let's just not stop.

"I-I can't. We can't." With a vigorous shake of her head, she takes another step back, dropping my hand, inserting space between us again. "I have a boyfriend, August."

Shit.

I shouldn't be surprised that she's taken. A girl this gorgeous, this funny and smart and authentic—she's all the adjectives I would use to describe the perfect girl for me. She's even the things I didn't know I wanted. But now I know, and I can't have her.

A hole gapes open inside of me wider and deeper than it should be considering how little I know about her, but it's there. And by the second, it fills with disappointment and lost possibilities.

"So . . . is it serious?" I wince internally. If there's anything more douchey than trying to kiss another guy's girl, it would be asking, in so many words, if she's sure she wants to stay faithful to him.

"Yeah." She sinks her teeth into her bottom lip. "We've been dating about a year."

She finally looks up at me, and at least the battle in her expression, the struggle reflected back to me from her eyes, assures me I'm not imagining the pull between us.

"I should have told you, but that would have been weird." She smiles ruefully. "I would have sounded like I was assuming you wanted more than . . ."

We stare at each other in a silence rich with things I shouldn't say.

"I *do* want more than." I manage a smile, though I'm frustrated and not just sexually. I'm downright devastated that some other guy got here before I did.

"I'm sorry." She stuffs her hands in the back pockets of her jeans. "I was enjoying our conversation so much. I didn't want to . . . I hope I didn't mislead you."

"You didn't." I stuff my hands in my pockets, too, to keep from touching her again. "At least I made a new friend."

Friend.

It sounds hollow compared to what I thought we could be, but I can't demand more. I can't *make* her give me more. I'm on the eve of something most men only dream of, and this bright-eyed girl has made me feel helpless.

"Yeah." Her face relaxes a little into a smile. "A friend."

"And you helped take my mind off tomorrow's game."

As soon as I say it, both of our eyes go wide. I check my watch, dreading the time.

Fuck.

Curfew.

Was I so absorbed by this girl that I forgot curfew before the biggest game of my life?

Yeah, I was.

"Oh my God." Her eyes are anxious, worried. "The game. You've missed curfew."

The hunger, the heat, the rightness between us had made me shove every other thought aside, but they all intrude now. *Curfew. The rest of the team, asleep and accounted for at the hotel. Tomorrow's game.*

"Will you get in trouble?" she asks, frowning.

"It won't be the first time I've had to sneak in," I tell her with more confidence than I actually feel. The biggest game of my life, and I lost track of time with a girl in a bar.

But what a girl.

Looking at her, replaying every moment, every joke, every memory we shared over the last few hours, I can't regret it.

"Let me at least walk you home." Curfew or not, there's no way I'm letting her go alone.

"No. I'm really close."

This part of the city is completely commercial as far as I can tell, not residential. "Your apartment is nearby? Or are you staying at a hotel?"

Does she live here? Is she visiting? A student? Is she in town for the game? Will she be there tomorrow? Does she want tickets to come see me play? All the things we *did* talk about are suddenly less important than all the things we never said. I don't even know her damn name. "Gumbo" won't get me very far after tonight. Panic tightens my body into a drawn bow. Even if it's never more than what we had tonight—the honesty, humor, ease, empathy— I want to continue with her. I'll even settle for the dreaded word —friendship.

"I'll walk you home," I insist.

"I'll be fine." She looks down at the ground and then back at me. The end is in her eyes. I see goodbye, and I want to stop it before it reaches her lips, but I don't.

"Goodbye, August. Good luck tomorrow." She turns and starts up the sidewalk.

I want to chase her. To follow and find out where she lives or where she's staying. Even knowing some lucky bastard found her first, I can't imagine having no idea how to find her again.

"Hey, wait," I call after her, forcing my feet not to follow. "You should at least tell me your name. Do you really want me to think of you as Gumbo forever?"

She faces me but keeps walking backward, steadily putting more space between us. Between this night and the rest of our lives. Mischief lights her eyes, and the sly smile playing around her lips makes me think for a terrible moment that she won't tell me.

"It's Iris," she calls back to me. "My name is Iris."

I stay still, absorbing the sound of her name, absorbing the look on her face as she walks out of my life with as little fanfare as she entered it. Her smile dies off, and she's staring at me like she wants to remember my face—like she won't forget tonight either. Like maybe, unreasonably, undeniably, this night meant as much to her as it did to me. If she felt it, too, this connection, she can't be walking away, but she is. I've only known her a few hours. It's unreasonable that desperation bands my chest and panic shortens my breath, like I'm sprinting.

Except I'm standing still. And she's still walking.

Walking and turning the corner, out of my sight.

She takes my hope for more with her when she goes.

***

Content Warning:

Please note that Long Shot has graphic depictions of intimate partner violence not involving the hero.
That content is not in the above excerpt,
but it is throughout the full novel.

***

All in Kindle Unlimited
Available Now

LONG SHOT (A HOOPS Novel)
Available in Ebook, Audio & Paperback
https://amzn.to/2PrMrqQ

BLOCK SHOT (A HOOPS Novel)
Banner & Jared's Story
Enemies-to-Lovers | Friends-to-Lovers | Second Chance
E-Book: mybook.to/BlockShot
Goodreads: http://bit.ly/HOOPSJared

HOOK SHOT (A HOOPS Novel)
Lotus + Kenan's Story
Ebook, Audio & Paperback
http://kennedyryanwrites.com/hook-shot/

Kennedy's Other Books

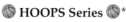 **HOOPS Series** *

(Interconnected Standalone Stories)

All Available in Kindle Unlimited

LONG SHOT (A HOOPS Novel)

Iris + August's Story

Ebook, Audio & Paperback:

https://kennedyryanwrites.com/long-shot/

BLOCK SHOT (A HOOPS Novel)

Banner + Jared' Story

Ebook, Audio & Paperback

http://kennedyryanwrites.com/block-shot/

HOOK SHOT (A HOOPS Novel)

Lotus + Kenan's Story

Ebook, Audio & Paperback

http://kennedyryanwrites.com/hook-shot/

All the King's Men Series*

The Kingmaker (Duet Book 1)

Ebook, Audio & Paperback

kennedyryanwrites.com/the-king-maker

THE REBEL KING

(Part 2 of The All the King's Men Duet)

https://kennedyryanwrites.com/the-rebel-king/

QUEEN MOVE (Kimba's story)

https://geni.us/QueenMovePlatforms

Reel (Standalone Book 1)

The Hollywood Renaissance Series

AVAILABLE NOW!

Buy: https://geni.us/Reel

A Hollywood tale of wild ambition, artistic obsession, and unrelenting love.

Directors. Actors. Producers. Costume Designers. Musicians. Writers.

A world where creatives make art and make love!

The Close-Up,

A Hollywood Renaissance/HOOPS Crossover Novella

Coming August 16 2022

mybook.to/TheCloseUp

Coming November 15, 2022

Before I Let Go,

Book 1 of the Skyland Series

https://geni.us/BeforeILetGo

THE SOUL Trilogy

Available in Kindle Unlimited

*My Soul to Keep (Soul 1)**

*Down to My Soul (Soul 2)**

Refrain (Soul 3)

THE GRIP Trilogy*

Available in Kindle Unlimited

Grip Trilogy Box Set: (3 Books in 1)

https://geni.us/GripBoxSet

FLOW (Grip #1)

GRIP (Grip #2)

STILL (Grip #3)

Available on Audiobook*

Order Signed Paperbacks

THE BENNETT SERIES

When You Are Mine (Bennett 1)

Loving You Always (Bennett 2)

Be Mine Forever (Bennett 3)

Until I'm Yours (Bennett 4)

Connect With Kennedy!

Twitter: @kennedyrwrites

Bookbub
Follow on Amazon

***

A RITA® and Audie® Award winner, *USA Today* bestselling author **Kennedy Ryan** writes for women from all walks of life, empowering them and placing them firmly at the center of each story and in charge of their own destinies. Her heroes respect, cherish, and lose their minds for the women who capture their hearts. Kennedy and her writings have been featured in Chicken Soup for the Soul, *USA Today*, *Entertainment Weekly*, *Glamour*, *Cosmopolitan*, *TIME*, *O* magazine, and many others. She is a wife to her lifetime lover and mother to an extraordinary son.

Printed in Great Britain
by Amazon

43940999R00119